Charming

METTE BACH

JAMES LORIMER & COMPANY LTD., PUBLISHERS
TORONTO

James Lorimer & Company Ltd., Publishers acknowledges funding support from the Ontario Arts Council (OAC), an agency of the Government of Ontario. We acknowledge the support of the Canada Council for the Arts, which last year invested $153 million to bring the arts to Canadians throughout the country. This project has been made possible in part by the Government of Canada and with the support of the Ontario Media Development Corporation.

Cover design: Tyler Cleroux
Cover image: Shutterstock

978-1-4594-1389-4
eBook also available 978-1-4594-1388-7

Cataloguing data available from Library and Archives Canada.

Published by:
James Lorimer & Company Ltd.,
Publishers
117 Peter Street, Suite 304
Toronto, ON, Canada
M5V 0M3
www.lorimer.ca

Distributed by:
Lerner Publisher Services
1251 Washington Ave. N.
Minneapolis, MN, USA
55401
www.lernerbooks.com

Printed and bound in Canada.
Manufactured by Friesens Corporation in Altona, Manitoba, Canada in July 2018.
Job # 245778

For Cathleen With for teaching and inspiring creativity

PROLOGUE

Viral

CHAR GILL WAS RIDING WITH HER MOM in the SUV. They had just loaded the car with stuff from Bed Bath & Beyond. Now her mom was chatting away about how she had to stage her next open house. She was explaining to Char how she used to hire stagers, but that it was easier to do it herself. Char's mom did everything herself, from manicures to taxes.

Char was staring at her phone.

"Put that away and help me navigate," her mom pleaded.

"That's what GPS is for," Char said.

"Do you even know how to read a map?" her mom snapped.

Char rolled her eyes. "Mom, this is important."

"So is making the right turnoff on the highway." They were on their way to the new outlet mall near the airport in Richmond. Char had tagged along because she wanted to check out shoes. But what was happening was way better than shoes.

"No, this is like, really, really important," Char insisted. She couldn't look away from her phone's screen. If she looked away, maybe it would all vanish.

"What is it?"

"Never mind."

There was no point in telling her mom. She wouldn't get it. There was just no way. But as they drove toward Richmond, Char saw her video get more than a hundred thumbs-up on YouTube in just twenty minutes. Everyone liked her cover of Rihanna's "FourFiveSeconds." At this rate Char would be famous before graduation.

That was the goal. That would set her up for a future. It wasn't just Char's goal, it was everyone's goal. But Char was the one on the path. And that was something she couldn't look away from for even a second.

01 All the Likes

CHAR TILTED HER PHONE EVER SO SLIGHTLY to the left. It was maybe her tenth try for a perfect selfie with her morning skim milk latte. She tapped on the cup with one of the fake nails she applied to hide her own bitten ones. It was hard to keep coming up with new stuff to post. The other girls at school seemed to find it easy. When you looked at their lives, everything seemed glamorous and beautiful. It wasn't that Char's latte wasn't good, but how could she get across how smooth and sweet it was? Or would be, when she could put her phone down and take a sip.

Char drove to school in her new orange Fiat. Her parents gave it to her when she got her licence. It came with a lecture on not being spoiled. But Char really needed a car in Delta. Everyone had a car. It was too far to walk to school and there wasn't a bus that went that way. She parked in the school parking lot and looked at the clock on the dash. Five minutes until homeroom. Plenty of time to sip the latte and check if there was any interest in her pic yet.

Not bad! Eighteen people in the time it took to drive from the Starbucks. Most were people she knew. But there were a couple of new people, drawn by her clever hashtags, Char was sure.

Weirdly enough, Mimi liked the selfie. Mimi didn't like stuff posted by people she deemed lower than herself in social ranking. All these people from other schools and clubs and things boosted her posts. Plus she showed a ton of skin, which got likes from lots of random pervs.

Mimi had also posted a pic. Twenty minutes ago, sure, but she already had more than forty likes. Char couldn't figure it out. Was Mimi buying them or something? No one really liked her, did they? Mimi was one of those girls you could never really trust. She'd be nice to your face and she'd like a picture every so often. But she never seemed truly happy for you.

Char didn't like to admit it, but it was taking a toll on her. She was forever chasing the one thing she couldn't seem to replicate. Her cover of the Rihanna song had been posted at just the right moment. It had more than a hundred thousand views. Almost overnight, Char had gone from being someone Mimi Jenkins had never heard of to someone she had to at least follow online. It's not that Char had magically been accepted in Mimi's circle — almost no one was. But at least Mimi said hi to her at school. And that was something.

But Char knew the pressure to upload stuff was getting in the way of other things. Of school and finding love and living a good life. Char used to go to queer youth events downtown or take part in the LGBTQ+ club at school. But it got too hard for her to defend herself for not being out. So now she spent all her free time thinking up ways to get back the excitement of instant fame. She'd never felt anything like it. Char, who had never done anything special, was a sensation. She had gone viral.

The problem with knowing that kind of bliss was getting it to happen again. Char never would have thought about it in the first place. But now she was showing the world her purchases at Lush, talking about the smell of bath bombs while she demoed scrubs on her hand. She had made a few videos of makeup tutorials and her evening skin care routine. But nothing passed one thousand views. What could she do to get those numbers back?

By the time two o'clock rolled around, Char was so tired from not paying attention in her classes that she was ready to go home for a nap. Good thing her last class of the day was music, the only subject she really enjoyed. She picked up her guitar and sat down. She began tuning just as Ms. Merchant entered, sipping from her commuter mug. It was clear Ms. Merchant shared Char's need for a ton of caffeine to get her through the day. And she made no pretense about it. Ms. Merchant lived alone downtown. She went out to hear a lot of local music and had a good sense of style.

"All right, everyone," Ms. Merchant began. "It's time to talk about the Seaquam Performers' Showcase and your year-end projects. For those of you pursuing careers in the arts, this is your big chance. You get an opportunity to perform live in front of an audience. You get a demo video shot of your performance and a shot at being voted best of the school. Not a bad way to end your last year."

Char looked around. A lot of kids took music because it made for an easy block. Aside from Char, there were a handful of students who were serious about music. Most of them probably also had other subjects they were good at or might have a future in. Char had to find a way to pull herself above the rest of them.

Ms. Merchant went on. "I expect that those of you who are serious about this are also nervous. That's a good sign. It means you care."

She looked right at Char. It was cool to have one person who believed in her. Her parents had signed up Char for piano and vocals summer camps for years. But they always told her that music was a hobby, not a career choice.

The class began to play and Ms. Merchant walked around, offering random comments. She was very careful not to hurt anyone's feelings. She had said early on that music was an art. She told them not to let anyone tell them they couldn't make music.

She stopped where Char was working out a chord series. "You know, Char," she said. "When I watch you play, I can tell that you've really got something."

"Thanks," Char said.

"If you keep working hard at it, one day you'll get there."

"Thanks," Char said again. But this time it felt like failure. She didn't like the idea of years of work ahead. That sounded too hard. She pulled out her phone to check on that morning's photo. Not too shabby. She was up to sixty likes.

02 Haters

THE BEAUTY VIDEOS WEREN'T CUTTING IT. Char was tired of describing smells and textures. She needed something to get more attention, more quickly. Another music video.

Char watched a bunch of Lilly Singh videos. The YouTube star from Scarborough was living Char's dream. Char knew she had to do things her own way, but she loved the high-energy vibe of Lilly's videos. She knew, though, that she could never pull off Lilly

Singh's natural thing. That would mean going without makeup.

Char spent a whole morning straightening her hair, perfecting her eyeliner, and getting her concealer just right. She was ready to try another cover. She grabbed her guitar. She made sure to position her phone to capture herself from above, the most flattering angle. She played an acoustic version of Camila Cabello's "Havana." Char had been practising it for a while. The hard part wasn't singing the song. It was the cute banter she needed to do before and after. It was looking cute and charming. She had to care just enough, but not too much. She had to balance goofy and serious. Once Char felt she nailed it, she posted the video.

Then it was back to fleece PJs and a ponytail.

Char looked through the comments beneath her video. She'd become used to a few thumbs-down and some talkback. But she wasn't prepared for what she saw.

Pathetic.

What a loser.

She'll do anything for attention.

She's so lame.

You suck. Why do you bother?

Why don't you end it?

That afternoon, still warm from her bath, Char curled up under a blanket on the couch in her room. She stared at the words on the screen of her phone. She knew that there were haters. She knew that any time you put something online, you risked trolls finding you. She knew that for all the people who took time to write something mean, there were probably more who watched, laughed, and moved on with their days. But still. Those words really hurt.

Char watched the view count go up to over a thousand. That was a big deal, since it had only been a few hours. It was not the time to think of herself as some sort of failure. This video was a winner. So why did the comments bother her so much? She couldn't shake it. She'd heard mean things before. But usually it had been the odd bad comment tucked in between several nice ones. This was different. It was like there were a whole bunch of people with the same opinion. And their opinion was that she sucked.

She put her phone down for a moment and stared out the window. She picked up her guitar and strummed for a bit. She pictured herself as a celebrity on late-night talk shows, reading out mean tweets directed at her. If she could get there, it would all be worth it. But what if she couldn't get there?

That night at dinner, her mom and dad talked about their work. Her mom was in real estate, and her open house had been a huge success.

"I'm sure we're getting multiple offers. There was so much interest."

"That's great," her dad said. "We could really use the good news after I spent all day at the new site." He turned to Char. "How about you? What did you get up to?"

"Oh, not much. I did my homework, played guitar for a while. Took a bath."

"God, I want to trade places with you," her mom said.

Char said nothing about the online comments. She knew better. Her parents had a vague idea that she posted stuff. But the one time she had alerted them to a bad comment, they completely freaked out. They made her delete the whole video. Everyone at school noticed the next day. It made her look like she couldn't handle having one idiot out there who said one little thing. So it was better to not talk about it with her mom and dad at all.

There were so many things her family didn't talk about. There was a reason that Char never brought up the fact that she was attracted to girls.

The online comments had turned into a full-fledged attack by Monday morning. Char nearly deleted the video several times. But she stayed glued to her phone. She'd been getting messages all weekend from people at school advising her in all directions.

Five friends, including her best friend, Everett, were on the side of taking it down. Six friends were on the side of leaving it up and letting it be proof of her popularity. Even if she did take it down, someone somewhere must have posted a copy of it. Then they'd get the views, not her. Char would get all the humiliation and none of the benefits.

In homeroom, Janice Watson leaned over. "Just so you know, Mimi is trolling you," she whispered.

"What?"

Janice nodded. "I'm not supposed to know. But I heard it from Chelsea, who's friends with Charice, who's friends with Alison, who was at the sleepover where Mimi was up all night coming up with all kinds of new handles. All the negative comments are from her."

"Why would she do that?" Char asked. She knew it wasn't that she was important to Mimi. Char was beneath her, wasn't even on Mimi's radar.

Janice shrugged. "Why does Mimi do anything?"

They shook their heads at each other.

Janice said, "You have to promise you won't tell anyone I told you."

"Okay."

"Because I'd die if she targeted me next."

03 *Weakness*

CHAR LOOKED AT HER PHONE ONCE MORE. She had stared at the meanness at home in her own space for hours. But if what Janice said was true, maybe there were some clues. It was awful taking in all that hatred again. And here at school, it was another thing. She could not — absolutely would not — show any sort of reaction at all.

And there it was.

The pop queen of Seaquam High.

So the commenter knew Char went to this school. She could talk to the principal if she wanted to make a big thing of it. But the principal would make Char and Mimi talk it out. He'd call their parents and make their parents talk it out. There might be some mention of it at an assembly. And she didn't think she could deal with all that. On the small chance Janice was wrong, Mimi would be so upset that she'd target both Char and Janice for sure. Mimi wouldn't have a hard time finding ways to make Char's life miserable.

On her way to Math class, Char passed Mimi and her friends in the hallway.

"Oh, hey!" Mimi said.

"Hey," Char said back.

"I hear you're famous now," Mimi said.

Mimi's friends started to giggle. One of the girls punched Mimi lightly on the arm. One of the other girls shushed her.

It was clear to Char. It was these girls who were

trolling her. Or, rather, it was Mimi.

As Char walked to class, she realized that knowledge was power at this point. It was better to hang on to the fact that Mimi was behind the trolling than to freak out and confront her or to tell on her. Besides, it didn't sting as much now. Now, she saw it for what it really was. It meant that she mattered to Mimi, online queen that she was. She was important enough for Mimi to be jealous of and come after. And that was what mattered.

Char knew she was addicted to the screen. No doubt about it. She was obsessing over what to post next, and what Mimi was posting. A ton of people at school liked Mimi's pics. Mimi knew that none of the people were her friends, and she didn't care. All she cared about was being popular online. Real life just didn't count as much. Char thought about how gross it was.

Char sat in Mr. Basra's classroom for homeroom. He taught coding, which was something Char knew absolutely nothing about. But she liked looking at the boards anyway. It was like looking at messages in a foreign language. Not a language she'd ever learn, but still.

Today she saw SendLove written on the whiteboard in red marker. There were some arrows pointing to the word *app*, and from there, another arrow to the word *cellphone*. She got curious and looked up the app in her app store. It was described as a way to battle online bullies, and it was brand new. Char hit "download."

Before long, she had the app open. All sorts of things were going on around her in homeroom. But Char was busy reading about SendLove. It was simple, really. She wondered why she'd never heard of it before.

SendLove was a place to go when you were being trolled online. You could tag places where your posts were getting negative comments. Other people on the app would send love. They could write all sorts of stuff to drown out the hate. The icon was a cool drawing of a girl in a cape, like a superhero.

It hit Char hard. She never thought of herself as being bullied. She wasn't a victim. But wasn't that what was happening? How did Char become a target? It was such a weird world to live in. You share something with people, just try to make them laugh or let them enjoy a song. Suddenly, all these trolls emerge and try to get you to shut up. Try to get you to stay in place, as if the world would be better off if you were silent.

Char loved the idea of the SendLove app. She wanted to sign up right away. But she held herself back. What if it got back to Mimi that Char had turned to people she didn't even know to defend herself? Mimi would read it as a sign of weakness for sure. And Mimi was an apex predator. Any sign of weakness, and Mimi would go in for the kill. Then Char would have an even bigger problem on her hands. No, she wasn't ready to sign up yet. But she was glad that such a thing existed. Knowing about SendLove felt like having a secret treasure.

Char knew deep down that social media was a bunch of smoke and mirrors. She knew that no one was as perfect and happy and beautiful as they showed themselves to be online. She knew it in her head. But she was almost always alone when she checked her phone, and often feeling down about herself. So it felt in her heart that everyone else had these beautiful lives. And she didn't.

But having something as private as SendLove made Char feel different. It reminded her that a beautiful life wasn't the thing that Char wanted the most. It wasn't fame either, though she was obsessed with improving her online stats. What Char wanted more than anything was to be able to be herself. She wished her online presence could reflect who she really was, not who she was pretending to be. Char knew there was something deeper inside of her begging to be let out.

04 Send Love

ONCE SHE GOT HOME, Char took off her studded leader jacket. She tossed it onto the couch in her room and flopped down next to it. Then she unzipped and took off the black leather heeled boots. The day was finally over. She sank into the plush cushion and sighed.

Char decided that she needed SendLove. She wanted to go on there to make her own comments on other people's videos and photos. It seemed like good karma. She signed up, calling herself Charming because it was just enough truth and just enough made up. Her parents had taught her the value of being liked — being charming. And her full name, that she never used, was Charmaine. She could hide behind this handle, but she could also be herself with it. Char took a picture of a ring in the shape of a crown, one of her favourites. She wanted something that was her but wouldn't be recognized. Of course she could have chosen a random photo, but she felt weird about that. She wasn't the kind of liar Mimi was. Char wouldn't make up fake accounts just to make it look like she had the power of numbers behind her. Besides, she'd spent her life going unnoticed.

Char spent the next couple of hours reading cries from girls who needed support. She did what she could, adding her two cents under this video or that photo. Lots of the girls were younger. Junior high, she figured. Some looked like they were even younger. She thought about what girls had to deal with. It should be easier, but it wasn't.

The moderator, Cinders, was on every thread,

cheering people on. Her icon was a picture of a pair of glasses. And she seemed to know what she was talking about. Char thought about the girls she'd read about or seen in the news, girls whose lives were made unlivable, who chose to end it all. She wondered if Cinders had that kind of background. This girl definitely seemed active and involved.

Char spent hours commenting and putting hearts under everything she could find. And she was surprised that she felt better about the world. This was a good thing, girls taking control. Banding together. Being strong.

She clicked on Cinders's profile and found that she could send a message to Cinders.

Charming: Must be nice to be so cheerful.

Then Char panicked. Why did she have to say that? It had seemed funny in her mind. But it wasn't funny at all. It sounded snarky. She felt like she was accusing this perfectly decent human of being shallow. The last thing she wanted was to hurt Cinders's feelings. Why couldn't Char delete it? Aaack! She was always doing this. She embarrassed herself by sending texts too quickly, revealing too much, going overboard. She always got accused of taking things too far. Her sisters and parents told her that. Everyone at school knew her as someone who didn't know when to stop.

The whole point of this app was to not say mean things online. And here she was saying something that seemed funny in her head but looked mean when she saw it on the screen. Char huffed. At least this person was a total stranger. Char was new to the app. She could disappear now.

Char went downstairs and had dinner with her family. By the time she came back upstairs, she'd forgotten that she'd made any comment at all. But there was a message in her new SendLove inbox.

Cinders: Just keeping it positive here. Believe me, not always cheerful. ;P

It was the goofy emoticon that made Char breathe a sigh of relief. She hadn't offended Cinders. Char went on the discussion board and realized that no one seemed to be judging anyone else. She felt accepted, even when she admitted that social media attention was really important — maybe too important — to her. When that comment sparked other people's stories, Char noticed how good Cinders was at making everyone feel safe. For the first time in a long time, Char felt like maybe there was somewhere she didn't have to worry about every word.

"So are you all set to apply for next year?" her dad asked.

Char cringed. She knew he wanted to show off that his daughter had a plan. It was like the way he showed off his new Apple Watch. Everything of her dad's was right on track.

"Not yet," replied Char. "I'm focusing on the

showcase at school. I'm going to use the video as part of my portfolio."

"Excellent, honey," her mom said. She was scrolling through her work phone.

"What are you applying for that a music video would get you in?" her dad asked.

"Um . . . maybe . . . the music program at Simon Fraser? Or, like, to try to get a job somewhere in the industry?" Char knew she was not convincing her parents. She was barely convincing herself. She should have thought this out better.

"We talked about this," her mom said. "You need to go to university for something you can turn into a business. You can't make a living as an artist."

Char sighed. To push the point would mean opening up the same old argument. Her dad would go on about starting off with nothing and working hard to provide this nice life for the family. Her mom would tell Char she was spoiled and expected everything to just be given to her. And there was nothing Char could say to that, because it was true.

"Are you going to do one of your covers for the showcase?" her dad asked.

Char was grateful for the shift in focus. "I've been thinking that might be the safe way to go."

"It's good that all those music lessons won't be wasted," her dad said. "I'm sure you'll beat the competition."

Char loved it when her dad seemed proud of her. But she suspected he'd rather tell his clients about it than actually watch her perform.

"You know, my mother was a good singer too," her dad added.

Char never knew her dad's parents. They had died in a car accident before she was born. They had left her dad and his brothers with some money, which they had turned into a real estate development firm. Char's dad's business savvy and her mom's great eye for staging made them the self-styled King and Queen of Real Estate. Char wished she'd known her grandparents. But she'd never been to India and only spoke English.

"But it wasn't music that paid for things," pointed out Char's mom.

Char thought about how her music videos seemed to be what people wanted. But could she become a real musician? She wanted to be the sort of singer that Ms. Merchant stayed up late for. The showcase was key.

05 Heroes and Villains

THE NEXT DAY, Char was on the SendLove app before school. She wanted to tag the negative comments on her latest video. She thought how great it would be for the SendLove community to deal with it. But she hesitated. Mimi probably checked back to see if her comments had any effect. And then she would wonder if Char had asked for help. Char didn't want to give Mimi that.

And there was something else. Char knew Mimi was always busy with her own accounts. There was one where she flirted with the camera and another where she made fun of everyone. These days Mimi was spending a lot of time picking on a girl who worked in the school cafeteria. Mimi called her Garbage Girl. How would that feel? Char wondered. It was one thing for Char to post videos and get trolled by the world. This poor girl was just living her life, and that made her fair game for Mimi's poison. How could Char go running to SendLove when there were real victims out there?

Okay, so "FourFiveSeconds" went truly viral. The Lush videos were at a few hundred views each. And "Havana" was going nowhere fast. How sad and pathetic. Char wanted to be better than caring about it, but she wasn't. Deep down, she knew that numbers didn't matter. If her song brightened someone's day, that was enough. She didn't need to be the next Rihanna. She didn't want to be Camila Cabello. Or Katy Perry. Or Taylor Swift. She just wanted to be herself and get known. *Ideally, for my music and charming personality*, she told herself as she put on her eyeliner.

Dressing for school was one of her favourite parts of the day. She never just threw on a sweatshirt. Oh, no. She made an effort. Nails done. Hair done. Makeup done. Colours coordinated. No holes in anything. Accessories. She liked to walk through the hallways and pretend that she was walking on a runway. You couldn't do that when you dressed like a slob.

That afternoon, as per usual, Char was the first one in music class. It's not like she tried to come early. Maybe the other students were slackers. In any case, it always seemed that Char had a few minutes alone with Ms. Merchant.

"Can I ask you something?" Char began.

"Sure," Ms. Merchant said.

"Why are girls mean?"

"Girl, if I could answer that," Ms. Merchant said, shaking her head. "That's the age-old question. Someone being mean to you?"

"Yeah, but she's kind of mean in general."

"You know, most people who bully have been bullied themselves."

"Yeah, I know." Char had read countless pamphlets and attended all sorts of workshops and assemblies on the subject. But that explanation left her wanting more.

"You know what the good news is?" Ms. Merchant asked.

Char shook her head.

"The good news is you're an artist. So you have an outlet. You have a way of expressing pain. A lot of people don't have that. They bottle it up and it comes out in other ways. Self-harm. Harming others. Music lets you deal with your feelings."

"I don't know about that," Char said. "Playing my guitar doesn't mean I won't get hurt."

"I never said that. You will get hurt. That's life. Life is full of pain. But you can take that pain and turn it into art. Have you been writing songs?"

"I've been trying."

"Well, keep at it. Doesn't matter if you're not writing about the bad stuff that's gone down. Actually, it's probably best not to. It'll come out in its own way, in how you process the world around you."

"Hmmmm."

"Art that really touches other people usually comes from some sort of pain."

Other students started to trickle in. Char was self-conscious about what she and Ms. Merchant had been talking about. So she searched through her bag for gum and pretended that she hadn't just had her mind blown.

Char couldn't get Cinders out of her mind. Well, why not contact her? When her invitation to chat on the app was answered, Char felt a tingle of pleasure.

Charming: Ugh.

Cinders: ???

Charming: My life. I'm kind of feeling like I'm not in the driver's seat.

Cinders: What happened?

Charming: I'm trying to figure out what I want to be. But I know I don't want to be what some people think I should be.

Cinders: Relatable.

Charming: And what if I change my mind? Everyone thinks that what's out there is the real me. And maybe it's not.

Cinders: I thought I was the only one. But maybe we're not talking about the same thing.

Charming: Sorry to be cryptic. Takes me a while to open up to anyone.

Cinders: Me too.

Char had always known that you have to plan your image, to make sure that people are seeing what you want them to see. Before she posted a video, she made sure that every hair was in place. Every expression was designed to entice. In the past, every time she sent out something without thinking, it came back to bite her. But this was different. She was working out what she was feeling as she was putting it out there to Cinders. Was this what Ms. Merchant was talking about?

Char and Cinders messaged back and forth into the night. And the next night, and many nights after that. Char found out that Cinders was seventeen, just like Char. That she had big dreams, just like Char. But it was the differences that gave Char a secret thrill. This girl wanted to change the world. And Char thought that maybe Cinders could change her world, if she let her.

06 Opening Up

"SO, UM, I KINDA MET SOMEONE," Char said to Everett. She opened her sandwich bag. "I mean, it's probably nothing."

Everett was chewing a bite from his apple. After a second, he said, "Oh yeah? Guy or girl?"

"Girl, silly," Char protested. "If there was a guy, it'd be you. You know that."

She punched him lightly on his arm. Everett had asked her out every year since they were in junior high.

And every year Char said, "It's not you, it's me." So here they were, best friends. Char worried that maybe it wasn't the healthiest choice for Everett. But she'd leave it up to him. And if he was willing to be her best friend, there was no way she was going to say no to that. Everett was one great dude.

"Where'd you meet?" he asked.

"Online."

"Does she live in Wyoming? Japan? What's the tragedy?"

"How do you know it's tragic?"

"Well, it's you." He laughed. "Have you ever had anything work out smoothly?"

"God! Why do I tell you anything?"

"All right, all right. Tell me about her."

"She's in high school. I don't know where. And she's . . . I dunno . . . she's different."

"Does she have six toes?"

"Are you jealous or something?"

He took another bite from his apple and looked away. That meant he was jealous. Char didn't want to push it. She knew what life was like without Everett. At the beginning, he had avoided her after being rejected. It was always lonely for Char at school without him.

"Anyway, forget it," Char said. "I'll probably never meet her. You'll meet some chick and I'll be your third wheel for decades. And then I'll die a virgin."

"Drama queen."

"I think it's being pretty realistic."

"Have you ever looked in the mirror, Char? No way are you dying a virgin." Everett laughed. "And just so you know, I'm not just talking about your looks. So don't accuse me of being shallow."

"Meh. I'm the one who's shallow these days."

"How?"

"I got to talking with this girl. I realized that some of the stuff I'm doing is maybe a little . . . I dunno . . . a cry for attention or something?"

"We all know you like attention." Everett smiled.

She shoved him again. "I guess. And I've been working on this song. But it feels like it's going nowhere."

"Song writing takes time."

"Yeah. I don't feel like I have a lot of that."

"Well, you do. We're young."

"I want to be big."

"Well, you know what to do. Work at it." He got up from the table where they were sitting. "That's what I'm going to do now. Hockey practice."

"Really? At lunch?"

"Yeah, it's just a few of us. Coach said we could." He picked up his tray. "See ya!"

Char waved at Everett's back as he left the cafeteria. Alone. Again.

She was checking her phone when a girl came up her table. It was the girl Mimi picked on. Garbage Girl. Their eyes met.

"Are you done with that?" the girl asked. She gestured to Char's tray.

"Uh, yeah," Char said. She thought about SendLove and wanted to say something. But how would this girl take it? Wouldn't it just be better for both of them to pretend they didn't know the bullying was going on?

It was time for Char to take a big step. She craved her nightly messaging with Cinders. She wanted more. It's not like she wanted to sext, though the idea put a smile on her face. She wanted to hear Cinders's voice. She wanted to see something more than the words popping up on the screen next to the picture of Cinders's glasses.

She got a little flirty with Cinders and then asked for her email.

Char held her breath. No answer. Then finally, an email address came through.

The first thing Char did was send Cinders a picture of herself. Char's face was in shadow and she was holding her guitar. Everett had taken it, and it seemed intimate. It was a picture of all the things that were underneath the jewellery and the makeup. Char had never felt close enough to anyone else to share it.

She couldn't wait for a reply, so she got on FaceTime and called Cinders, voice only. After the first awkward words, Char was surprised that they got right to things she had never admitted to anyone, not even herself.

"I've always made music," said Char. "Singing, piano. I love my guitar, as you can see. But it's only been lately I've wanted to have a career in it."

"But how are you going to support yourself in the meantime? I mean, most artists need day jobs, at least at first."

"Duh! I'll sponge off my parents." Char laughed. "Truth is, I'm totally scared about that part. I feel like there's no way any kind of McJob is going to be enough to float me." Did that sound like she was spoiled?

"No?"

Char was thankful that the one word was not snarky. It sounded like Cinders really wanted to know. "I'm working on some other avenues. Passive income, that sort of thing."

"That's cool."

"But I'm kind of scared I'm not very good."

"At singing?"

"Singing, songwriting, playing guitar," sighed Char. "All of it. I'm pretty good at performing. I don't mind an audience or a camera."

"I can't stand attention. Can't do public speaking. Makes me feel like I'm going to die."

"Really? How do you get by? Like in school and stuff."

"I just do whatever I can to stay out of the spotlight, even if it means doing more than my fair share of group work or whatever."

"I find it hard to relate to that."

Cinders laughed, but in a good way. "I can tell. I'm glad, because it kind of sucks. I wish I was more like you."

"Hmmm. And here I am wishing I was more like you."

By the time they finished, it was three in the morning. Char was ready to curl up into a ball and sleep for days.

The next day, the conversation continued through SendLove chat. At school, at home. There was back and forth all day. All the pretending Char did had worn on her, and she was desperate to let her real self be seen. She began talking about what made her feel insecure. Before she knew it, she was telling Cinders everything, even things she never told Everett.

Charming: So I'm afraid of not being good enough as a musician. I'm scared that even if I give it my all and put in the years it'll take, it'll go nowhere.

Cinders: Where do you want it to go?

Charming: I want to share what's in my heart. I want to play for audiences and inspire people. Would I like fame and money and record deals? Hell yeah. I'd be lying if I said I didn't.

Cinders: Every artist wants to be recognized.

Charming: Maybe that's just it. Maybe I want recognition more than I want to do something good for the world. That's kind of pathetic, isn't it?

Cinders: I don't think so. It's okay to want feedback, to feel like you're part of a give and take.

Charming: Maybe that's what it is. Thank you. I've been hard on myself about wanting attention. But maybe it's just that I want some back and forth.

They chatted long into the night again. Char learned that Cinders's mom had recently died. Char felt bad for Cinders. *How small my problems are compared to that*, she thought.

The funny thing was that Char felt good about herself while she was online with Cinders. And she wasn't used to that. She had conversations all day, every day, at school or online. But she always felt like she had to live up to other people's standards. And she felt she failed at that. Cinders made Char feel like it was okay just to be Char. Too bad Cinders was just someone online, someone Char would never meet in real life.

07 *Mirror, Mirror*

LIKE MOST DAYS NOW, Char found herself walking around the halls like a zombie. No amount of coffee could keep her awake. She went to the cafeteria for more anyway. The girl who worked there also looked like she'd been up all night. Or maybe she was just tired from working. Char nodded as they went through the motions of getting a coffee fix. The girl rang up her order. A large coffee. Char produced a toonie and change. Then she went to the counter to add four packets of sugar and a whole lot of cream. That would carry her through until lunch. After that, she had music.

In music class, Ms. Merchant got everyone to talk about what they planned to do for the showcase. They went around the room in a circle, counter-clockwise. Char knew she'd be last to speak because she was seated to Ms. Merchant's right. She listened while everyone came up with their ideas. Inside her head she critiqued their choices. A lot of the singers were doing vocal acrobatic R&B numbers like you would see on *American Idol* or *The Voice*. A couple were doing hip hop, complete with dancing. Char's eyes glazed over when the musicians went on about their instrumental solos.

"I want to do a pop cover," Char said when it was her turn.

"Not the one from YouTube?" one of Mimi's friends said. The girls beside her giggled.

"You know you're good at pop covers," Ms. Merchant said. She shot a glance at the girls who'd laughed, but they ignored it. "But what about stepping out of your comfort zone? What about challenging yourself to write something original?"

Char felt weird being singled out and asked to step up. Everyone else was allowed to do covers. But that seemed to be the point. Ms. Merchant wasn't treating her like she was everyone else. Char had never been teacher's pet in any class. She always scraped by on God knows what. So it was a big deal to her that Ms. Merchant was on her side.

"Yeah, maybe," Char said slowly.

When she got home, Char sat in her room. She looked at a little glass bird that sat on her windowsill. Her mom's parents had got it for her in Tivoli when they took her there to explore her Danish roots. She held the delicate glass up to the light. She stared at the blending of yellow and turquoise for a long time.

She lost herself in the moment. And somehow, she started to hear music. A melody and some chords crept into her mind. She got out her guitar and played the first phrase of a song. Then words came too. They weren't lyrics — yet. But they came out of nowhere and they matched the chords.

That night, Char talked Cinders into FaceTiming with video. It was great hearing Cinders, but Char wanted to let Cinders see her. Not her face or anything. Char didn't want to pressure Cinders into revealing too much too soon. But Char wanted to show Cinders who she was right now, without cleaning her room or setting up things to make herself look cool.

Once they were on video, Char didn't hold back. She wasn't quiet and she wasn't afraid. She didn't show Cinders her face, but she revealed a whole lot of other stuff. Char showed Cinders around her room. She showed Cinders her guitar, even played a bit for her. She got kind of bossy and dared Cinders to flash her. She was shocked when Cinders almost did. It wasn't exactly a flash, but there was definitely skin. It was super hot. Char was tempted to "slip up" and face the laptop cam, show her face. But she didn't want to scare Cinders away.

Everett met Char at her locker. The two of them walked together to the cafeteria. It was important not to go into that lion's den alone. They decided that the best spot was near the recycling and bussing stand.

Mimi and her friends trailed in at ten past noon. They walked like they owned the place. As if the illusion of power was enough, a group of grade elevens vacated the table next to Char and Everett to make room for them. Mimi and company talked really loudly. Char tried to ignore them.

"So yeah, I think I'm going to take the job," Everett said. He looked at Char for a second. "You haven't heard a word, have you?"

"What?"

He shook his head at her. "Earth to Char. Quit obsessing over them." He tilted his head at Mimi's bunch.

"I'm not obsessed."

"When did Mimi post her last photo?"

"This morning at 7:48."

"How many likes does it have?"

"I haven't checked in a while. Eighty-eight last I looked."

"When was that?"

"Right before lunch."

Everett grabbed Char by both arms and looked her straight in the eyes. "You have got to stop competing with Mimi. She is awful. You're above this and you know it."

"Do I?" Char pouted.

"Yes. You do." He was firm. "If you don't put an end to it, I will."

"How?"

He shrugged. "I dunno. Turn her in for that stupid bullying Instagram account? Tell the truth about how she trolled you?"

"Shhhhh." Char put a finger to her lips.

"Why are you protecting her?" he asked. And then, to no one in particular, he asked, "And why do I not understand girls at all?"

"I can't help you there," Char said. "I've done everything in my power to help you understand the female mindset."

He smirked at her.

Char smirked back, then got serious. "I just can't stand how she acts so high and mighty. And how she'll do absolutely anything for attention."

"Well . . ."

"What?"

"Nothing."

"Oh, come on. You were going to say something. What?"

"I guess I'm thinking it takes one to know one."

Char let that sink in. Then she went to slap him. "What the heck is that supposed to mean?"

"Nothing." He put his arms up in defense.

"Explain yourself, mister."

"Do I really need to? I mean, you've seen your own Instagram, right? And your YouTube channel?"

"I'm not like Mimi," Char huffed.

"Well, you don't expose other people on a mean blog or anything."

"But?"

"But you do care way more than you should about

how many people like your stuff. And you always compare it to how many people like hers."

Char snarled like a caged animal. "Goddammit. I hate it when you're right."

"Then you must hate things all the time." He chuckled at his own joke.

Char knew things needed to change. The song that came to her the other day, that was the future. That was what she wanted. This stuff with Mimi was petty. Everett was right. It was beneath her.

They ate their lunch in silence for a bit. Then Char asked Everett to back up to his story about getting a job. This time, Char actually listened.

08 Unplugging

CHAR WAS TROUBLED. She had spent the night going over in her mind all her recent online activity. She messaged Cinders and they agreed to FaceTime again. Char felt like she was a different girl from the one who had flirted with Cinders just two nights before. The first thing she did was make sure that Cinders didn't regret anything about knowing Char.

"I'm really disappointed in myself," Char went on. "I feel like I've been shallow in a lot of ways."

"What do you mean?"

"I think I've bought into everything I know is wrong. Like being popular. Image. That kind of stuff."

"I don't even have time to think about that stuff. I guess that's why people make fun of me. But I barely have time to listen to their insults. I just focus on my work."

"You are so cool. Do you know that?"

"Me? Cool? That'll be the day."

"Cooler than most. You must know that."

"I try not to compare myself with others."

"Are you serious? How do you not do that?"

"I dunno. I just don't. I focus on the stuff I'm working on. When I'm at work, I focus on work. At school, I focus on school."

"I get the picture," Char said. "You make it all sound so logical."

"It just makes sense. Comparing yourself to others will only make you unhappy."

"Thanks, Yoda. What else ya got?"

"That's it. I'm sure you'll figure it out. You always do."

"How do you know that? Maybe you don't know me that well."

"Don't I?" Cinders asked. "I feel like I know you pretty well."

"Okay, maybe you do. But what do I do to stop the addiction? I mean, I'm totally obsessed with my online presence and chasing fame and all of that."

"I'm not sure. Other than SendLove, I'm not on social media enough to cut down on it myself."

There was a pause. Char pictured Cinders, living a real life, not one online. Char wanted that. But would she be able to do it?

"I think I should unplug for a while," said Char slowly.

"Wow. Sounds very . . . severe."

"Not really. My parents have a cottage I could stay at for a week. There's no Internet, and I'd leave my phone at home."

"Okay, well, whatever."

"I'm serious. I think maybe what I need is to detox from the house of mirrors that is social media. You know how you look at other people's lives and you can't help but feel like you're doing everything wrong?"

"No . . ."

"Okay, not you. But most people, Cinders. Most people."

"So how will we stay in touch?"

"I guess we won't. I guess we'd have to take a break from talking."

"Oh. Um. Okay."

"Is it? Is it okay?"

"I guess it has to be. You've made up your mind."

"I just need to get out for a while. You get that, right? It's not you. If I could stay in touch with you and not have any of the other stuff, I would. But I don't know if that can happen. I feel like I need to do this."

"I understand," said Cinders, and Char believed her. "I'm just going to miss you. That's all."

"I'm going to miss you too," Char choked out. Cinders had no idea how much.

It hadn't been hard for Char to persuade her mom and dad to let her take a week off school. She told them she needed the time to get her school applications done.

On the ferry, Char was talking with an elderly couple.

"Where are you off to?" the woman wanted to know.

"My parents have a cottage on the north pier," Char answered.

"You're going by yourself?" the man asked.

"Yeah," she answered. What was the problem?

"We live up that way," the woman said. "We can give you a lift if you want."

"That'd be great."

Char had left her car at home, along with her phone. It seemed the right thing to do. She had food and everything she needed in her backpack. She had planned to walk to the cottage, just as she'd done every time she'd gone there alone. But a ride was much better. After all, it was misty out. She'd be wet to the core by the time she got there if she walked.

"It's beautiful this time of year, isn't it?" the woman said. She looked back at Char from the front seat of their old station wagon.

"It really is," Char agreed. She felt the weight of Delta fall off her. All the pressure to fit in and be cool slipped off like the drops of water from her raincoat. On the island, she felt like she could breathe.

The man's voice snapped Char back from her thoughts. "You know, we saw a pod of orcas near the north pier just the other day. I wonder if they're hanging around."

"Wow. Really?"

"Yep. A mama and her calf and, well, the whole pod."

"That's so cool." Char said. "I haven't seen orcas since I was . . . Oh, it was a long time ago. Maybe two years?"

The couple both laughed. "Is two years a long time ago?" the woman asked. Then she patted her partner on the arm and said, "I guess we're in trouble."

"I didn't mean anything by it." Char had done it again, said something stupid. But here, it didn't seem to matter. The words just floated away, instead of being caught onscreen.

"Oh, we know, dear. Everything is different when you're young."

They pulled up in front of the dark cottage. Char had second thoughts about staying all alone. But she reminded herself she'd done it before and it would all be fine.

"Thank you so much for the ride," Char said.

"No problem," said the woman. "If you need anything, just holler."

"Seriously," said the man. "We can probably hear you from here."

They all laughed.

Char unlocked the front door and reached for the light. It was cold inside. But that wouldn't take long to fix. She turned on the heat and started to boil some water.

Time passed very slowly on the island. Without a phone, laptop, or tablet, Char felt completely lost. It was like she wasn't herself at all. And then she realized that in fact she absolutely was herself. It was the digital version she needed to let go of.

09 What's Real?

THAT NIGHT, SHE SLEPT like she hadn't slept in ages. It was partly the quiet, partly the fresh air. It was the real dark that you never got in the city. The smell of trees. All of it made her so sleepy that she went to bed at nine and slept until nine in the morning.

When she got up, she made coffee and looked out the window at the foggy day. She stood, wrapped in her blanket, and sipped her coffee slowly. Everything took forever here. There was no need to multi-task.

She had time for it all.

After breakfast, Char got dressed. There was no point in wearing makeup. But she still felt weird about going without it. She was so used to wearing it that she was naked without it. Then it struck her — that was a problem too. She never questioned it back in Delta. But here, she questioned everything.

She made a thermos of tea. She locked the front door and began the trek down to the bay. That's where the couple had said they'd seen whales. If Char did nothing all day but wait for them, it would be a good use of her time.

Char stood near the shore, out on a pier. She took in the stillness of island life. Her parents had talked about moving here, but she and her sisters had protested. Now Char wondered how different her life would be if the family had made that choice. She poured some tea and thought about Cinders. Char wanted to reach out to her, wanted to have her there with her.

And then, out of the corner of her eye, she saw a

faint splash. She was pretty sure she knew what it was. She looked out into the misty grey. She could see nothing. Slowly, her eyes adjusted to the light. It was bright despite the fog. Char felt like she was engulfed in a cloud. Then, a couple of minutes later, she saw it again. There was a splash and then another. Tiny droplets of water burst up toward the sky like from a fountain. Definitely the blowholes of orcas. She knew the sound. She waited and watched. It felt as if they were testing her. It was like they were trying to decide whether they should reveal themselves or not. Char kept quiet and waited.

The dorsal fins emerged. Char looked out over the black and white whales. She could see the arched back of the mother. And there was the calf. They were playing in the bay. She watched them for a long, long time. All of her worries about school and fame and being popular faded to nothing. Char was completely at peace. She still longed to talk to Cinders, to share this experience with her. But she knew that they would connect. And she understood that some things are meant to be experienced alone.

As Char walked back to the cottage, she had the feeling that everything would be okay. She wondered if she loved Cinders. Could it be possible to have such strong feelings so quickly? The feelings were real to her and that was all that mattered. She had never been in love before. She had nothing to compare it to. All she knew was that she wanted to share everything with Cinders. Those nights they talked were everything to Char.

As soon as she was back in the cottage, the music came. Char grabbed the old guitar they kept there. It was out of tune and a pretty cheap one to begin with. It was nothing like what she had at home, but it didn't matter. The music flowed through her. She wrote and wrote that day. There were no words, but the music spoke of water and mist and orcas. Char wasn't tired. She was in awe.

That night, as she heated some canned soup and made toast, Char pictured a life with Cinders by her side. A life like this one, not back in Delta. Maybe they could move to the Yukon together. Or to the

Australian outback. Or to Costa Rica. Char pictured them spinning yarn and making jam. She wanted to live off the land and be in touch with nature. She wanted to forget about all the shiny offerings of the city.

And that was when Char truly felt like she was free of Mimi. Char didn't want to be like Mimi. Not one bit. Everett was right. Comparing herself to Mimi was a mistake. She would stop it at once. From now on, Char's focus needed to be her music and her love. That was all that mattered.

Char lit a candle. She thought about telling Cinders about all of this. She wrote words on a piece of paper she found. When she was done, she folded it up and stuck it into her backpack. The words of the song would be about Cinders. Even if they never met in person, Char would live with the knowledge that her soulmate was out there. The only thing in their way was the screen.

Back on the ferry and then on the bus to Delta, all Char could think about was contacting Cinders. Char didn't care about anything else. She longed for their chats, longed to tell Cinders what she'd seen and felt. She wanted to make Cinders feel as if she was there with Char. Because, in a way, she had been. Would it be weird to ask Cinders if she'd sensed it because she'd been in Char's heart the whole time? Maybe a little obsessive, Char figured, but also the truth. She had to tell Cinders that she was falling for her.

When she was finally back at home, Char tried to FaceTime Cinders. But Cinders didn't come online. Char kept checking. No sign of her yet.

"Yeah?" Char called when there was a knock on her bedroom door.

The door opened. It was her dad. "We're ordering in from Cactus Club," he said. "What do you want?"

"Umm . . . butternut squash ravioli?"

Just as her dad left, Char got a FaceTime call. It was Cinders.

"I've been thinking about you. About us," Char

said as soon as she answered. What was the point of hiding? There were times in her life when she'd tried to play cool. But she had no time for it now.

"You have?"

"Yeah. Like a lot."

"I've been thinking too. Here's the thing. I need to focus. I have so much going on right now. So much work and school."

Char felt like she was crushed under the weight of those words. In all her life, she'd always been the one who rejected. Being on the other side of that was the worst.

"Me too. I'm busy too," Char said. It wasn't a lie. The showcase was coming up. But Char knew she would drop everything in a heartbeat for a chance to meet Cinders in person.

10 Showcase

THE CAFETERIA LOOKED like a concert hall. There were mics and amps and monitors. There was a bank of lights set up near the stage. The drama teacher, Mr. Ramirez, had set up a video camera to record the performances. It looked totally pro.

Char stood at the back and watched her classmates do their thing. She was short of breath, and her chest was tight. She loved an audience, but this was something else. This was more than an audience. This was her future. If she was going anywhere with her music, it would be because of her voice and sound, not her grades. She had to make it count.

Ms. Merchant sat near the front with a clipboard on her lap. She was taking notes the entire time. That made Char even more nervous. Ms. Merchant was nice about things in class. But to be on a stage and have a teacher judge, that made Char anxious.

When it was her turn, Char's insides constricted like she was going to be sick. But she knew she had to look as if she owned the stage. She walked up with the kind of confidence she saw in old footage of Tegan and Sara. She nodded to the audience and to the camera. Then she sat down on the stool.

Knowing what was coming made it really hard. She hadn't really told anyone that she was queer. Everett knew because he knew everything about her. And she guessed that some teachers suspected. She thought maybe a couple of students had their ideas about her. But she had never really said it. There was something about saying it that would make it so. There would be no way back from some words. And here was a song all about it.

The music Char had written on the island came together with her note to Cinders. It was like magic, and it put Char right back at the cottage. She sang about Cinders. She sang about their connection and how it made her feel. She sang about falling in love with this girl's words, her voice, and the way her mind worked. She sang, knowing her own feelings in spite of not even knowing what this girl looked like. The biggest surprise for Char was how great she felt. The music was like the Force in the Star Wars movies. It went through her and all around her. It bound everyone in earshot together. Meshing what she felt at the cottage and how she felt about Cinders made the song bigger than herself, bigger than her life. Even before the song was over, Char wanted the feeling of singing it for all those people again.

As Char finished the song, Ms. Merchant took a tissue from her purse and wiped her tears. The audience cheered. They weren't even supposed to. They barely clapped for anyone else, and that applause had been forced. This clapping was different. It was real. It was from the heart. It was like everyone listening could tell that this was important. It was a big deal, not just for Char, but also for everyone. *It's always a big deal when someone tells the truth*, Char thought.

Char picked up her guitar and exited stage left. She fished a bottle of water out of her backpack and downed it. She suddenly realized she was hungry as well as thirsty. Before going on stage, she hadn't even thought about eating. But now she craved something. She wanted more — to make more music, to have people listen to her more, to talk to Cinders. But all she could think about was getting something to eat.

It was loud in the cafeteria. All those people were talking to be heard above the hum of fridges and beeps from the music gear. Char went to the menu board, ordered a sandwich, and waited to pay. The cashier was the girl Mimi was always picking on.

"I heard your song," the girl said. "It was amazing." Char could barely hear her voice and was mostly reading her lips. The girl had nice lips.

"It really sounded okay?" Char asked.

"Yeah. I couldn't work while you were singing. I had to stop everything and listen."

"Thanks," said Char. "That really means a lot."

"That'll be eight dollars and ninety-five cents for the sandwich," the girl said, pointing at the display.

"Oh, yeah," Char said. She rummaged through her backpack for her wallet. Time had stood still for a second there. *It must be the high from being on stage*, Char thought, as she stuck her credit card into the reader and keyed in her PIN code.

"Thanks," the girl said. She handed Char a receipt. "You were great."

"You too," Char said. Then she heard the words she'd spoken out loud. She shook her head at herself because they made no sense. She hoped maybe the girl didn't hear her. "I mean, thanks."

What the hell was that? Char wondered as she scouted out a spot to sit. She had probably made a fool of herself, spacing out like that. But she couldn't bring herself to really care. She sat down to eat her sandwich.

Within minutes, she was surrounded.

"Well done," Everett said. He dunked a french fry into a paper cup of ketchup. "Good vocals too."

"Thanks," Char said. She was a bit surprised that he was cool with it. She had just come out in front of the whole school and confessed her love for a girl. Maybe he'd made peace with the fact that no amount of chasing her would ever get her to go for him.

"It's a good angle, too, you know?" Everett munched away.

"No," Char said. "I don't know. What do you mean?"

"You've been talking about how you want to increase your subscribers. Boost your platform and all that."

"Yeah?"

"Do I have to spell it out for you? The world loves lesbians."

"That is not true," Char declared. "Not true at all. Maybe at your house. Not at mine."

"I don't mean our parents. I mean out there."

He gestured all around. "Even here. You got applause. Nobody else got applauded."

"Sure, but . . ."

Janice was sitting within earshot. She turned on her bum to face them. "I couldn't help overhearing, so I'm barging in. Hope you don't mind."

Char kind of did mind. What was with people and their opinions? But all she said was, "Yeah?"

"If you really want to make a difference, get famous first. Then come out."

Char didn't respond. What the hell did Janice know about any of it?

"I'm serious. Look at Kristen Stewart, Miley Cyrus, Ellen Page, and Demi Lovato. They were all famous first and then they came out. I bet they wouldn't have become famous if they came out first."

"I don't know about that," Everett said. He loved debating.

"No, it's true," Janice insisted. She looked right at Char and said, "You just hang on to that song and songs like it until after you hit the big time. You can go far.

But only if you leave your options open at the start."

"Do you really think so?" Char was amazed that Janice thought she could be a success. She barely even thought about the other stuff she was saying.

"I do. You just have to project the right image. And you do. Like, I never would have known."

"That I'm queer?"

She nodded. "Yep."

"I'm not sure what to say," Char said. "I mean, thanks? I think?"

It was troubling praise, that was for sure. What did it mean in Janice's world to look queer? What kind of image did she have of LGBTQ people? Janice, who wore bulky sweaters and had probably never been outside of Delta, was hardly the kind of person Char would ever take fashion advice from.

11 *Trolls*

"CHAR, YOU WERE GREAT UP THERE," Brittany said. Mimi stood right behind her. Mimi was listening to everything, but didn't look up to make eye contact with Char. She fixated on her phone.

"Thanks," Char said. She sensed that Brittany wasn't being sincere. She just wanted to do what everyone else was doing, coming up to Char and saying nice things.

"Oh my God," Mimi said. She grabbed Brittany

by the arm and rammed her phone in Brittany's face. "Look!"

Brittany exclaimed, "Oh my God."

Everett, Janice, and Char all sat dumbfounded. Suddenly, they were an audience. Mimi's audience.

"What?" Janice asked.

"Oh, never mind," said Mimi. "You wouldn't get it."

Everett made a face. "Okay." The sarcasm was clear. But Char knew that Mimi didn't pick up on stuff like that.

"It's just that, like, I just got retweeted by, like, one of the bachelorettes."

"Oh my God," Everett said, mocking her. "I'll alert the press."

Mimi didn't listen to him. She was too busy squealing about her tweet.

"What did you actually tweet?" Char asked.

"Oh, you know, some thoughts on the show."

Char didn't know how else to respond. A few weeks ago, she would have been impressed or at least intrigued. Now Mimi struck her as desperate. Char could see what was happening with new clarity. Mimi could not handle Char being in the spotlight even for a second. Char had sung something that people were talking about. People were coming up to Char and praising her. That was like poison to Mimi. It was her undoing. She needed all attention on her at all times.

The showcase had taught Char that all eyes were on her. For better and for worse. She might as well make it for the better. She went through her medicine cabinet and her junk drawer in her bathroom. She had so much crap. All sorts of half-used lotions and potions. Palettes where the colours she'd liked were gone and the colours that remained made her look like a clown.

She applied her eyeliner. She wasn't going anywhere and she already had liner on. But she was pretty good at eyeliner, so why the heck not?

Char got out her video camera and set it up. She didn't overthink it. There wasn't any point. She'd been practising a Charlie Puth song for a while now. She thought she was doing an okay job. Their vocal ranges were close. It had been forever since she had slapped something up online.

Char talked at the camera and made goofy faces. Then she grabbed her guitar and got down to it. She got it shot in less than fifteen minutes. Some quick editing and she had it up before dinner. The song was about being into a girl. She wondered if that would make her seem too queer for YouTube. After all, it wasn't just the school this time. But when Char thought about the showcase, sadness and self-doubt crept in with the memory. She had hoped that making this video would capture the magical way she felt on stage. But it all felt kind of flat, no matter how many subscribers she had or what kind of comments it might get.

After eating with her parents and sisters, Char went back upstairs. She checked on her video.

Amateur. She can't even sing.

She looks like shit.

Ugh. Barf!

Gay!

That word.

Everett was wrong. The world did not love lesbians.

How could one silly video get so many negative comments in such a short time? One answer: Mimi. She must have set an alert to search for all new content. Only someone from school would make the jump from one song about a girl to full-on "gay."

That night, Char wanted to reach out to Cinders. She wanted to tell Cinders that knowing her had helped her see things in a different light. Cinders was so honest and real, she made Char see that online fame and friending and fandom were kind of empty. It was as different from connecting to real people as making a video was different from singing to a real audience. Char realized that genuine was better. And she wanted to be a better person. For Cinders. But the last thing she wanted was for Cinders to think she didn't respect Cinders's work, her focus. Char put down her laptop and picked up her guitar.

The next day, Char was walking down the hallway at school when she saw Mimi and her gang up ahead. She thought about changing direction. But they'd already spotted her, and she didn't want to seem weak. Instead, she did a mental check of her posture and the expression on her face. She pretended she'd just received some great news. She took a deep breath and kept walking.

The girls all stared at her. She felt the weight of their gazes. She wondered if they were extra interested in her because they saw her queerness as something to mock. She had lost respect for their stupid games. As Char passed them, one of them blurted something familiar.

"Amateur."

Now Char knew for sure. Mimi and her gang were the trolls. She thought about Cinders, and it was just enough to keep her walking instead of turning to their awful troll faces and punching them. They put on their perfect makeup and tried to live up to some perfect image. But Char saw right through all of it. They cowered behind namelessness and threw rocks at someone just for putting their art into the world. They really were monsters.

And what was the best way to deal with monsters? It was to not believe in them. Her parents had taught her that. When Char was little, she had thought there was a giant lizard that lived under her bed. She had been scared until the night her parents gave her a flashlight. They had told her to inspect the darkness any time she wanted. She had planted the flashlight on the floor and left it on all night. Every time she woke up scared, she'd lean over the edge of the bed and take a peek. And sure enough, there had been no lizard.

Char had to shine a light on these girls once and for all. They didn't matter when she was on the island. And they didn't matter when she thought about Cinders. They weren't a part of that. And they probably couldn't understand true love.

But she didn't say anything to them. There was no point in setting herself up to be targeted even more.

12 Royalty

PROUD OF HERSELF FOR FACING MIMI without relying on SendLove, Char logged in and checked the registry. The app community had grown huge. It was now impossible to respond to every request for support. It would be a full-time job to follow up on each case of a girl being targeted. That was a depressing fact. Char didn't know why the world was so cruel to girls who put themselves out there. But she did sense that it wasn't personal, that none of it had anything to do with the actual girls. That was an even sadder thought.

She checked in with Cinders through SendLove. They hadn't agreed to be out of touch entirely. And she really needed some perspective from someone not deep into the drama at school.

Charming: Can you chat?

Cinders: I am working, but yeah. I'll FaceTime you in a bit.

Charming: I'll be right here waiting.

Char felt like she was putting all her cards on the table by typing that. Love was a funny thing. No one wanted to come across as being needy. No one wanted to have high hopes, in case they were sent crashing down. Maybe it was best to be guarded. But Char didn't like those games.

She tried to do her math homework, but couldn't focus. She scrolled through her phone and followed some SendLove requests. Mindlessly, because she couldn't engage with each one, she made little hearts appear under people's posts.

Finally the little box came up on her laptop screen, and she saw the dark window into Cinders's room at night. She felt a flutter in her belly. She was always nervous talking to Cinders. She wanted to be her best. But she was also relaxed in a way she had never been with anyone. Because Cinders always saw her best. It was funny, like fitting two complex puzzle pieces together. It was so obvious she and Cinders were more than friends. But they also connected like the best friends she'd ever seen.

"Where've you been hiding?" Char asked.

"I've been around," Cinders said.

"Are you mad at me?"

"Why would I be mad at you?"

"I figured maybe you were done with me."

"Just the opposite," Cinders said. "Actually, I think about you so much that it makes it hard to work sometimes."

"Then we should be connecting," Char said. "Because my life is so much better with you in it."

There was a pause. Char tried to keep from panicking. There was no taking back what she said.

Their talk went back to a safer topic — SendLove. Char couldn't figure out why Cinders was on it all the time when she had said she had too much work to do. Then Cinders turned Char's grasp of reality upside down.

"I created SendLove," Cinders said.

Silence. *What. The. Hell*, thought Char.

"You whaaaaa???" Char was floored by what she'd just learned. SendLove had changed Char's whole relationship with social media. Just like Cinders had changed Char's whole concept of what it meant to be real. This one person had done all of that. As they talked more, Char learned that Cinders didn't even see the app as a big deal. Char had to step away for a bit. She said, "I have to pee. I'll be back in a sec."

She went to the bathroom and looked at herself in the mirror. She ran her hands through her hair. She got really close and looked at the blackheads around her nose. She saw all her own flaws larger than life. And all she could do was stare at herself and wonder what she could offer someone like Cinders.

She ran back into her room and said in the direction of her laptop. "I'll just be a minute. Hang on."

Cinders said it was fine. Char thought she heard Cinders talking to someone as she was leaving the room. But all Char could think was that the girl she liked made the rest of them look like trash. Cinders wasn't online to create the fake queendom that Mimi aspired to. She was the real deal. All her life, Char had seen people grabbing at fame and attention. Even her parents, the King and Queen of Real Estate, plastered their faces on bus stops and their services on billboards. And here was Cinders, humbly plugging away. Doing the right thing. Being an actual leader. Cinders had real royalty.

Char grabbed her phone, went back to the bathroom, and closed the door. She put that morning's towel at the bottom to make the room as soundproof as could be. Then she got into the bathtub, which was dry now, thankfully. She drew the curtain shut and called Everett.

"What's up?" Everett asked.

"Dude. You have got to help me."

"Where are you?"

"In the bathroom."

"And you're calling me?" he laughed. "Who do you think I am, a doctor or a kinkster?"

"Listen. I just found out that Cinders is a much bigger deal than I thought. I mean, I knew she was a big deal because I've been falling for her. And, well, I was about to ask her to meet me. But then I learned that she's a seriously big deal. Not just to me but, like, in the world."

"Is she a Kardashian or something?"

"Get real. She's a programmer."

"Oooh. A programmer."

The sarcasm in his voice sent Char over the edge. "Why did I even call you?" she cried.

"All right, all right. So you're freaking out. And you want me to tell you to stop freaking out, right?"

"Kinda."

"Stop freaking out."

"That's it?" Char asked. "Not good enough. Tell me something else."

"Like what? That you're good enough? That she'll agree to meet you?"

"Yeah, yeah. Stuff like that."

"Char, this shit is scary. Believe me. I've been in your shoes. Remember?"

"Oh God. Don't remind me."

"If she rejects you, she probably won't be as mean about it as you were to me."

"Uh . . . thanks?"

"She won't reject you. Why would she?"

"Why wouldn't she? I'm totally beneath her."

"Based on what standard? You're being irrational."

"No, I'm finally seeing things clearly."

"You're being insecure," he said. "And I have to say, there's a part of me that really likes seeing this side of you."

"Oh screw off."

"No, I'm serious. I don't mean it like you think, though. I've never seen you like this before."

"What am I like?"

"Vulnerable. You really want this."

"Like I've never wanted anything."

"Yeah, this side of you is totally new. You're in love."

"Am I?"

"Yep. And it hurts."

"Nice pep talk."

"Hey, you put me through the ringer for four years. I get to see you seeing what it was like to be me. Don't take that away from me."

"Fine. Fine. Continue."

"It's a horrible nightmare," he said.

"Thanks," she blurted.

"But it's also the best thing ever."

"How?"

"Because it is. Don't you feel alive right now in a way you never did before? Aren't you seeing the world in colour when it used to be black and white?"

"Yeah. All of that."

"So that's great, right?"

"It is if she wants to meet me. What if she doesn't?"

"She will."

"How can you be so sure?"

"Because, Char. Because I am certain."

"I'm sorry I ever put you through the ringer, Ev."

"You didn't know what you were doing. You'd never been in love before."

"Oh God. Stop using that word."

"Char, nothing else would make you do the crazy. You are squatting in your bathtub, calling me at midnight."

"Oh God. Oh God. She's still on FaceTime on my laptop. She's sitting in my room just waiting for me to emerge. I'll have to explain why I was in the bathroom so long."

Everett laughed. "Get back out there."

"Hey," Char said. "I love you. Not like that, but like, you know."

"I know. I love you too, Char. Now go get your girl."

13 So Close

"HEY," CHAR SAID, as she took her spot on the bed with her laptop open and facing a poster on her wall. "Sorry about that."

"No big deal," said Cinders. "I just solved something on SendLove and then started on something else."

"Of course you did," Char said. She didn't laugh out loud. But she was amused by the difference between them. Char was having a breakdown in the bathroom. Cinders was pulling a Bill Gates.

"I should get going," Cinders said suddenly.

Char knew that it was time to live up to her handle. She had to charm Cinders. Cinders was as shy as a half-tame animal. And Char couldn't afford to let Cinders slip away into the forest. She had to keep her talking. Char knew that she wanted friendship with Cinders. She wanted romance with Cinders. She wanted it all.

"So, um, you know how we've been talking for a while now?" Char said.

"Yeah?"

"Don't you think it's time we let our guards down a bit?"

"I guess." Cinders sounded doubtful.

"Like, what part of the world do you live in?"

"Fine. Canada."

"No way! Me too," Char said. "I should have known you were Canadian."

"Why?"

"Hello. Awesomeness."

Cinders laughed.

Char said, "I'm on the West Coast."

"Me too," Cinders said.

"Get out!" Char said.

"I'm by the border," Cinders said. "Are you somewhere cool like Kitimat?"

"No. Like you. South."

"I live in the suburbs."

"Of Vancouver? Or Victoria?" Char asked.

"Oh, God. I don't ever tell people stuff like this. Of Vancouver."

"Me too! I'm in Delta."

"Delta? How can that be? That's where I am."

"No! What school are you at? You better say North Delta Senior Secondary or I will completely lose it," Char said, holding her breath.

"Seaquam."

"No! That's my school."

"Are you serious?"

"Dead serious. Home of the Seahawks."

It was fate, then. Char's heart was about to pound its way right out of her chest. She was in utter shock. Who was this girl who lived and studied right next to her? Right alongside her? Where had she been hiding and how had they not met?

"We have to meet," Char said.

"Um. I don't know."

"For real? All this stuff in common. And this weird cosmic connection we have. And you don't know if you want to meet up?"

"I'm shy?"

Char shook her head. "What are you afraid of?"

"Honestly? Everything."

"Yeah. I get that. Me too."

"Really? Because you don't seem afraid."

"Are you kidding me?"

"You don't. You seem kind of fearless."

"Well, I'm not."

"I don't know. It's worse that we're at the same school. I don't like who I am at school. Or who I've been made out to be."

"Does anyone?" Char asked. "I mean, I don't either. I'm getting by okay. This year is better than last. I'm looking forward to the whole thing being over."

"Me too. I just need to focus. That's the other thing. I like talking with you, really, I do. But I'm working on this project that's taking a lot of my time. The augmented reality project."

"Oh yeah?"

"I guess it came out of losing my parents. My idea is to use Google Glass technology to preserve footage of real people who've gone. Even create new footage. What if we could put on glasses and see those people right in front of us? Or you could fill the space around you with works of art."

"Sounds like something out of sci-fi."

"If we could go back in time twenty or thirty years, people then would think that how we live now is sci-fi. Things keep changing."

There was a long pause. Char tried to hear the sound of Cinders keying. But there was only silence. Char was trying to think of the next thing to say. It had to be perfect. It had to let Cinders know how desperately Char needed to keep their connection. To let it grow.

When Cinders started talking again, her voice

changed from full of hope to sad and resigned.

"Charming, I have to stay on top of that change. I have to do whatever I can to change my life, just to survive. So I don't have time to get involved with anyone."

Char was stunned. Cinders couldn't be saying what she thought she was.

"So that's it then? We're over before we ever began?" Char choked out.

"I have to go," Cinders said in a really quiet voice.

Char felt a wave of pain start in her chest and cover her whole body. She felt sad and angry and frustrated all at the same time. "Fine," she said. She logged off before Cinders had a chance to say anything. Char didn't want to watch the little window disappear. She'd always been the last one to log off, and there was always something painful about it. Maybe Cinders was right. This whole thing was just some stupid fantasy. They were better off never knowing if they had a future.

14 Putting It Out There

WHEN CHAR GOT DRESSED FOR SCHOOL, everything felt off. She couldn't find that joy she normally felt in choosing the right outfit to match her mood. Char settled on her royal blue cardigan, blue jeans, and boots. Everything blue made sense to her. There was nothing hopeful in this.

It was painful to think that Cinders went to Seaquam. How could they be so close and yet so impossibly far away from each other? Maybe Cinders didn't actually go to this school. Maybe it was Mimi messing with Char all along. That would be a pretty evil thing to do to a person. But if anyone was capable of it, Mimi was.

The hallways were full of people. Yet Char felt utterly alone. In the sea of faces, anyone could be Cinders. Or maybe Cinders was no one at all. Char really didn't know what to believe.

"So . . ." Someone tapped her on the shoulder. She turned to see Everett smiling at her. "What happened?"

"Ugh. The worst."

"She rejected you?"

"She doesn't even want to meet me. And she goes to our school. Can you believe that?" Char threw herself into Everett's arms and started to cry.

"No, actually," he said into her hair. "That's pretty strange. Are you sure?" He patted her back and held onto her as she sobbed.

"I mean, she said Seaquam." Char sniffled. "It seems weird to me too. What are the odds?"

"But if it's true, she can't be that hard to find. I mean, just piece together the clues. What do you know about her?"

"She works a lot. She's a coder. She invented an app called SendLove but she's totally secretive about it. I saw it written on the board in Mr. Basra's classroom. Actually, that's how this whole thing got started."

"You can find her."

"So she can reject me to my face?"

"Maybe if she knew it was you. If she knew you . . ."

"No. I have to convince her to want to meet me. I can't just show up in her face. She wouldn't want that. I wouldn't want that. It's not cool."

"Yeah, I guess it's a bit stalkery," Everett said.

"Unless she's going to ghost me entirely, I can probably find her online and . . ." Char couldn't finish the sentence. She didn't know what to say.

Char moved through her classes like a zombie, half dead inside. At school, at home, she was barely able to take anything in.

By the next day, she was a mess. She sat with her back against her locker and took out her laptop. She wrote Cinders a message.

Charming: I could be wrong about this, but I feel our connection is deeper than any I've had with anyone else. I don't want to distract you from your work or get in the way of your goals. But I do want to meet you because I think love is pretty rare. And if you haven't guessed already, I have fallen for you pretty hard. Maybe that's a weird thing to say since we don't know each other. Sometimes I think this is all some cruel joke. But then I remember the sound of your voice and I know you are real. I believe that. Please let me get to know you. In real life.

She read over the message many times. It was too much and not enough all at once. She didn't send it. She didn't want to seem like a stalker.

When she was home from school and safely in her room, she read it again. She knew if she sent her feelings out into cyberspace, she could not take her words back. But she knew that if she didn't tell Cinders how she really felt, she'd regret it forever. She didn't want to live that way, always wondering what might have been. Better to put herself out there.

Once she'd sent it to Cinders's inbox, she wanted to take it back. She wanted to say other stuff. Say less. Say more. Nothing was right.

She kept staring at the screen for hours. No sign from Cinders at all. Finally, she noticed that Cinders was online, so she sent an invitation to chat.

Charming: I guess you're done with me?

Cinders: How've you been?

Charming: Good, I guess. Were you ever going to get in touch with me again?

Cinders: I've been busy.

Charming: This doesn't feel like a real relationship.

Cinders: I guess it isn't.

The words on the screen seemed cold and distant. Where was the Cinders that Char knew?

Charming: I'm calling you.

Char switched to FaceTime, praying that Cinders would answer.

"Hey," Cinders said. She was almost whispering.

"I don't even know who's ghosting who at this point," said Char.

"I meant to call you. I've had all this stuff to deal with."

"I thought maybe you don't want to keep this up. Maybe the only reason you ever did was because of one random night online," Char continued.

"That is not true."

"Feels true."

"Things aren't always what they feel like."

"No, but sometimes they are."

"I feel alone," Cinders whispered. "Alone and worried about things I can't even talk to you about." Her voice was almost breaking. It was a far cry from the cheerful Cinders Char had first found on SendLove. It broke Char's heart.

"What's going on?" she asked.

"I'm starting to think that I'll never get out of here. I feel like my whole future is at stake. I thought making SendLove would help. But here I am, a victim of online bullying."

"I hate the Internet," Char said. "It's ruining my life, too. But back to you."

"I hate that I care. Because I honestly don't really care what other people think. I just want to get the hell out of here. SendLove people are doing what they can. But it's not enough and that's such a depressing thought. When will it ever be enough?"

"When people stop hating on each other."

"When will that happen?"

"Honestly? Probably never."

"I don't have time for this. I have actual goals."

"So achieve them. Stand up. Claim SendLove. Whoever it is will leave you alone when they realize they're messing with the wrong person."

"You think?"

Char thrilled at the small hope in those two words.

"Of course. You have to do this."

"What about the haters?"

"Helloo-oo? Your app is all about that. I mean, if anyone has something to teach haters, it's you. You have something to share with people who are the target of haters. What's the worst that can happen?"

"Being targeted doesn't scare you?"

"I can think of worse things." It surprised Char that now, she really could.

"Are you for real? What could possibly be worse?"

"Oh, all kinds of things. Like being told to stay in the closet. Or being told that the world loves lesbians and to hurry up and be out. Fighting with your parents. Having no idea how to have a career. I'm sorry. That's my shit storm. Let's talk about you more."

"No, what's going on with you?"

"Uh, well . . . I don't know how much of it I can tell you. At least right here, right now."

Cinders sighed. "This is why I feel like this is going nowhere. We can't talk about anything anymore. If we ever could."

Char knew that all she had to do was show her face to Cinders. Cinders would see how much she cared. She wanted to step into the shot framed by the cam. But she couldn't. All the trust they had built up would be crushed into a million pieces. Maybe there was another way. "That's not what I'm saying, Cinders. What I'm asking is if we can meet in person."

"Really? I didn't think that would ever happen."

"I was getting afraid that it would never happen."

"What's changed?"

"Everything. All the stuff I used to be afraid of doesn't scare me anymore. Instead what scares me is the thought of letting you go. Of letting this pass us by."

"What is this?"

"I think we should find out. Meet me at Brown's on 64th and Scott in an hour. Please." Char held her breath.

"Okay," Cinders said. "I'll be there."

15 Garbage Girl

CHAR DROVE TO THE STRIP MALL COMPLEX with the Safeway and a pet food store. Brown's stood off to the side. It was a boxy building with long slim windows that seemed out of place in this neighbourhood. As she parked, she changed her mind once more whether it was a good idea to meet so spur-of-the-moment. She and Cinders had agreed to meet. But now that she was actually here, she second-guessed everything. Were they supposed to meet inside? Should she wait in the car? She flipped down her mirror and checked her makeup. There were beads of sweat across her forehead. She dabbed them away with a tissue. They were replaced by new ones. She wasn't wearing her jacket or anything.

She rolled down her window and stared all around. Nothing. There were people getting in and out of their cars to go to Safeway and the liquor store, but that was about it. Nothing else was open. This wasn't the kind of strip mall where people loitered and smoked. There was no point staying in the car. She couldn't sit and wait forever.

Char walked to the entrance of the restaurant, deeply aware of the clacking of her boots on the asphalt. She opened the dark brown door and looked inside. There was a family waiting to be seated and a couple that seemed to be together. No girl her age by herself. Char still secretly feared that the whole thing was a set-up by Mimi. That it was designed to ridicule her on camera and get the video on her evil Instagram account. All Mimi cared about was clickbait.

It also occurred to Char that Cinders might decide not to show. She could have freaked out, or she could have come to her senses. She hadn't sounded like she wanted to come.

Char paced back and forth. A woman with long, beautiful lashes in heavy makeup greeted her with a smile. "For one? Or are you meeting someone?"

"I'm supposed to be meeting someone. She's not here yet."

"Okay, so I'll put you down for two. It might be a few minutes."

The place was hopping even though it was a weeknight. There were very few places to go, so everyone came here.

"All right," Char said. She felt out of place. Tense. Crowded. "I might just go wait outside for a bit."

She went out again. Hovering by the entrance gave her the feeling of being in the way somehow. Where could she go? She paced back and forth. She should look in the windows of other stores. If and when Cinders arrived, Char could walk toward her from the closed produce store. Maybe it wouldn't seem weird because Cinders wouldn't know that Char had been hanging around trying to kill time.

Char walked all the way to the market. There was nothing to see at all. She turned and still saw no one. *I've really been stood up*, she thought. But then the bus pulled up along Scott Road. When it turned onto 64th Avenue, she saw that there was a girl her age standing to exit the bus. The girl was wearing the glasses Char saw every time she was on SendLove. Char walked to the bus stop with her hands in her pockets.

"Charming?" the girl asked.

"Cinders?"

She was not at all what Char expected. The girl standing in front of her was not someone she had ever noticed at school. Char's mind ran through the cliques she knew, but couldn't place this girl in one. But Char knew she had seen her. She was familiar, but not. She was pretty in a plain sort of way, like a movie star before she gets famous. This girl was the sort of person one could overlook in a crowd. The weirdest thing was that she seemed fine with that.

"You're Char Gill," said Cinders. "I was at your showcase performance."

"Oh, yeah." She was the girl who had sold her a sandwich. She was the girl that Mimi kept posting pictures of. "You were working. You said some really nice things about my song."

Cinders laughed. "Yep. That's me. My name's Ashley, by the way. Call me Ash."

Char put her hand out, like it was a formal moment. They shook. "I can't believe you were there while I played a song about you," Char marvelled.

"That song was about me?" Ash was still holding her hand.

Char was suddenly too shy to look Ash in the eyes. She nodded. "There's only so many people at our school. I knew you couldn't hide from me forever," Char said.

"That's what I was afraid of," Ash said. "You'd see me and know you were up late chatting and FaceTiming with Garbage Girl."

How could Char tell Ash how precious she was to

her? "That's so not what you are to me. Or to anyone. Cinders, I mean Ash. Let's go inside. It's too cold to deal with this out here."

As they turned to walk toward the restaurant, Char was a bundle of nerves. She had wanted this moment for so long. She didn't know what she'd been expecting — fireworks and streamers and fanfare. Instead, it felt super real. Here was the real Cinders. Ash. Char could talk to her, look at her, and maybe even hold her hand. Funny, she'd been able to go much further on FaceTime. But now she was with Ash in person, that world felt far away.

They sat across from each other in a dimly lit restaurant. Ash seemed lost in her own world.

"What are you thinking about?" Char asked.

"I just can't believe the song was about me. I'm replaying that moment in my mind. And, well, it was so beautiful."

"I'm so happy you were there to see it."

There was silence again. But now that Ash was there, Char didn't dread the silence.

"So your handle," Char said. "Charming isn't much of a stretch. But why Cinders?"

"Cinders. Ash. Makes sense, right? My mom was into mythology. She named me after the phoenix rising from the ashes."

Char thought that Ash's name was perfect. She thought Ash was perfect. She was getting lost in just looking at her.

Suddenly she realized that Ash didn't seem comfortable.

"I shouldn't be here," Ash said.

"Why not?"

"I don't belong at a place like this."

"What? Here?" Char looked around.

"Yeah."

"I don't see the problem."

"You really don't? You're not looking, then. You feel at home in a place like this. I can't. You're way more everything than me. Popular, pretty, confident."

"Don't do this to yourself, Ash. You are hands

down the smartest person I know. And the craziest part of all is that you're so humble about it."

Ash became tearful. "It's hard to hear that you believe in me. We're just very different. Aren't you friends with Mimi?"

"God, no. Can't stand her."

"I thought you were friends. She's always talking about you."

"To you?" Char was surprised.

"Not to me so much as near me. I live with her and Noah. I'm their stepsister."

It all seemed so wrong to Char. The best person on the planet was living with horrible people. She wanted nothing more than to rescue her.

16 Kiss

A SERVER WHO LOOKED LIKE A MODEL came to the table. "Can I get you two something to eat?" It broke into the little bubble Char and Cinders had built up around themselves.

"Can we get the social sodas, but, like, mocktails instead of cocktails?" Char turned to Ash and said, "They're delicious."

Char shifted her focus back to Ash. She was clearly hurting. No wonder she hadn't wanted to meet anyone from her school. No wonder she focused solely on getting out, graduating, and moving on.

"I'm glad you're here," Char said. Char could not imagine what Mimi was like to live with. What it would be like to have her posse come over and be in your private space.

"You are?" Ash asked.

Char tried to express to Ash how special she was. "I've never met anyone like you. You are who you are and that's so cool. And you're so not trying to be cool."

"You're right about that," Ash said. "I accepted not being cool a long time ago."

"Which is what makes you so cool."

Ash scrunched her face up and scowled. Even her scowl was cute. "You think?"

"I can't believe you. Look at SendLove. You created a cure for online bullying. Do you have any idea how amazing that is? And you don't want to make money or fame off it. You're a really good person. I didn't know there was such a thing."

"You didn't?"

"Hell no. Everything around me is toxic. My family is a mess. Even my so-called friends. Other than my friend Everett. He's cool. But I'm so done with this scene. I just want to do my own thing now."

"You will. You have to. You have such a beautiful voice all on your own. I was blown away that night I first heard you."

"When I sang about you." Char smiled.

After eating, they took a walk down 64th and Wade Road into a little park. It was funny to be at a playground at night when all the kids were at home sleeping. Char and Ash sat on the play structure that looked like it could be a pirate ship, or just a regular old boat.

"It's so incredible that you're real, that I can sit here next to you," Char said. The cold night breeze made Ash clutch her arms around herself. Char wanted to put her arms around her too.

"You seem cold."

"It's chilly."

"Can I hold you?"

"Yes," Ash said.

Char reached her arms around Ash and cradled her. Why had she never reached out to this girl in real life? She flashed back through the times their worlds had collided. Mostly, it had been at the cafeteria. But sometimes they had passed each other in the hallways as well. How had Char not known that her soulmate was right there, living a parallel life right alongside her?

She pulled away and took Ash's hand in hers. They both stared at each other.

"I really can't believe you're here and that we've sort of known each other all along. I mean, not really known-known. But you know what I mean," Char rambled. She wished she could stop but she couldn't. "It's just strange that we've like walked right past each other and never known."

"Yeah," Ash said. She looked shy. She looked like

someone who didn't know what to say.

Char had the opposite problem.

"Because all this time I was building up this idea of who you were by your voice and your presence online. I mean, you know, I read everything you wrote on SendLove and kind of stalked your every move. Not in a creepy way. Well maybe a little bit in a creepy way. Oh God. Why can't I stop talking?"

"Because you're nervous."

Char looked into Ash's eyes. The eyes that could see things for exactly what they were. It made Char even more afraid. She gulped. Looking into Ash's eyes was like being truly seen. She had never felt that before.

"Can I . . . uh . . ." Char fumbled. She stopped. She was afraid. But somewhere she found the courage. "Can I kiss you?"

Ash nodded.

Char leaned in closer. So did Ash. Their lips met and Char melted into the softness. She put her arms around Ash and held on tight. She felt she was about to tip over. She couldn't think. All she could do was feel.

"Let's get out of here," Char said. "My car's back at the parking lot."

They walked in silence. They stole glances at each other and smiled. When they approached the bus stop where Ash had walked into Char's life, something came over Char. She took Ash by the arm. They locked eyes. It was like they could speak without words.

Char kissed Ash again. This time, she was much more forward. She had never French kissed anyone before. It always felt so weird to think about two people twisting their tongues together. It looked confusing in movies, like you could easily screw it up if you weren't careful. But instead of thinking about it, all Char wanted was to do it. She guided Ash back a step so that her back was against the wall of the bus shelter. Then she leaned into her and the tongue thing just kind of happened. It was amazing. It was perfect.

They kissed like that up against the bus shelter until their lips were chapped. Char had never experienced anything remotely like this. Char was dizzy. Light-headed.

"I believe we were heading to my car," Char said. She grabbed Ash by the hand and tugged on her gently. They walked hand in hand to Char's orange Fiat. It was a lot like floating, the way they walked. It was as if their feet barely touched the ground.

Char unlocked the car by pushing on the key, but she went to the passenger side and opened the door for Ash. Ash got in.

"Thank you," Ash said as she got in and did up her seat belt.

Char sat in the driver's seat and took a breath. She needed a pause before she could focus on the road. She looked at Ash who had her hands on her lap. Ash closed her eyes and Char put the palm of her hand up to Ash's cheek. Ash leaned into the cradled hand and tilted her head slightly. They kissed again. Tongues twisting, necks straining. The whole thing seemed like a feat of magic, like they shouldn't be able to move like that.

"Let's go to my place," said Char. "My parents are asleep by now. And they wouldn't care anyway."

Char didn't wait for Ash to say "Okay" before starting up the car.

17 Heartbreak

CHAR DROVE THE FAMILIAR STREETS, but everything felt different. She was sure nothing would ever be the same again. She could not undo this. She remembered the time Everett had asked her if she was sure about her sexual identity. When she had said she was, he wanted to know how she knew, and she couldn't explain it. There was a good reason for that. It needed no explanation. It just was what it was. She wondered why people didn't ask about straight desire. That was never questioned.

She parked in the driveway of the house she'd lived in all her life. She was used to having people over. Everett came over all the time and her parents didn't even notice. But for some reason, this was different. Char was nervous. If she did see her sisters or her parents and they asked, she didn't know if she would call Ash a friend or what.

They didn't run into anyone. Char opened the door to her room and turned on the light. The overhead light seemed too much, too soon, after the darkness of the park, the bus stop, and the car. She tossed her coat on her chair and turned on the lamp on her bedside table. Then she came back to the light switch and turned it off. She took Ash's hands in hers.

Ash was still wearing her coat. She had little beads of sweat on her forehead.

"I'm sorry. Here," Char offered. "Let me help you." She held Ash's jacket by the collar as Ash snaked her way out of it. Char threw it on top of her own coat, looking at how their outer layers co-mingled. She hugged Ash. "I'm so glad you're here."

Ash let out a sigh and looked off into the distance.

"What are you thinking about?" Char asked.

"Oh, nothing."

"Come on. Tell me."

Char guided Ash to the bench that was built in to her bay window. They leaned against the cushions in shades of grey.

"That I can't do this." Ash said.

"Do what?"

"Be with you," she said quietly. "It's not you. It's me."

"But, Ash, you don't even know me."

"I know that you're in a different sphere from me. I don't belong in your world."

Char looked into Ash's sad eyes. For the first time, she saw Ash looking frightened. Char thought she was the scared one.

"Is it the queer thing?" Char asked. Because that sure was scary.

"No, it's not that," said Ash. "I mean, I wish I'd had a chance to tell my mom. I know she'd be cool with it. She was cool with anything."

"So then it's me?" Char wanted to cry. She held it together, but she felt exposed. Maybe she was a bad kisser. Maybe she was too forceful. Too hopeful.

"No, not you," Ash said. "Just kind of . . . everything." She looked down at her feet. "I don't know how to tell you. Mimi's not totally wrong about calling me Garbage Girl. I take pop cans to the recycling depot. I literally peddle garbage."

"But that's not who you are."

"Who am I then?"

"I see someone who is trying her best to get out of a bad place. I see someone who is smarter and brighter than people see. But you know why? Because you won't let them. If you would let people see you, they would."

"I know you think it's weird I'm not more out about the SendLove thing, but . . ."

"It's not just that. It's everything. You could own the whole Garbage Girl thing. If you got all up in Mimi's face about it, what could she say? Squat all. You know why? Because she's a spoiled little princess and you're not."

"She's got her problems."

"I can't believe you're defending her. It's so amazing that you do that. No one else would. I'll tell you one thing. If I had to live with her, no way could I be as nice as you. That's the thing about you. You have a perfect heart."

Char raised her hand above Ash's left breast. She held the palm of her hand there and felt the heart beat deep within Ash. Ash looked down at Char's hand. She put her own two hands on top of it.

Char wanted to kiss Ash one more time. She leaned in, but Ash pulled back.

"It's not you," Ash said. "Trust me when I tell you it's not you. I have to go."

She grabbed her coat and was out the door.

Char could still smell the scent of Ash's hair in the room. It was a floral, fruity note with a hint of spice. The room felt empty. It lacked the heat and warmth that had just been there. Char sat on the bench and cradled her knees to her chest.

Why?

She wondered if it was worse to have met Ash. How could she face her at school now? Char would have to ignore her. She would have to stuff the feelings down and pretend it was okay. But nothing was okay. She started crying.

Ash said it wasn't about her, but how could it not be? Didn't everyone want to find love? Wasn't that the whole point of life? It was the message in every movie and book. Char's whole life had been practice for this moment. But she had bombed. Love had come and gone in just a few hours.

Char was struck with how perfect Ash was. She had been right there all along, and Char had seen her. She just had never looked at her like that. But now she could. What were the odds that their lives would intersect like this? And how could it be possible for it not to mean anything? Every word, every moment they had shared that night replayed itself in Char's mind. None of it added up to the truth of what had just happened. Ash was not supposed to leave. This was not how it was supposed to end.

Char had never been so confused in her life. When the sobbing finally stopped, she dabbed her eyes with her sleeve. It was just past midnight and she was alone again. The only thing she wanted was to have Ash back. But that wasn't going to happen. So she did the next best thing. She took her guitar on her lap and she played.

Out of her misery came some of the saddest heartbreak songs she knew. She sang "Hurt," trying to put all Johnny Cash's world-weary heart into it. Then something inside of her stirred. This tragedy could make her get into bed and not get out for weeks on end. Or she could bleed her feelings into her music. There was really no choice. Words and melodies, bits and pieces came to her as if from far away. But it was also as if they'd been inside her all along. She didn't know where the music had been hiding, but it was making its way out. And somehow in releasing it, she felt better. Her heartbreak wasn't going anywhere. But being able to express it lightened the heavy weight in her heart just a little. She thought about Ash wanting to use augmented reality to keep her mom's love in her world. Maybe Char could use her music to do the same thing. Maybe her music could keep a bit of Ash in her life.

Before Char knew it, it was five in the morning. She had filled pages and pages with words and chords. As she crawled into bed, she thought about how fiercely she wanted Ash to sleep next to her. She wanted the feeling of Ash's body behind her, pressing into her. She longed for that feeling so much that she propped her extra pillows into the shape of a person and leaned up against the heap. She pretended it was warm and that she had Ash's arms around her. Their first real kiss had been so passionate, Char had been left dizzy. Now she was so tired and so sore in her heart and her lips that she wanted it all to end.

18 Underneath It All

CHAR WOKE UP THE NEXT DAY to her dad knocking on her bedroom door.

"You alive in there or what?" he called before poking his head in.

Char groaned and pulled the blanket over her face.

"It's past noon," her dad said.

She groaned again.

He came in and picked up the papers scattered all over her room. He rifled through them. "What's all this?"

"Nothing. Just some songs I was working on."

"I didn't know you were doing that."

"I wasn't. I'm not. I don't know."

"Come down and eat some lunch. I almost hauled you out of bed earlier, but your mom told me to let you sleep."

"Thank you," Char said. "I'll get up."

She changed into sweats and a hoodie. In the bathroom, she splashed water on her face.

When she came out, her dad looked stern. "Who is Ash and when did you start kissing boys?" he asked in a dark voice.

"Um, Dad, it's not what you think." *If only it was that simple*, Char thought.

"Do I need to call his parents? What's going on? Does he go to your school?"

Char sighed and sat down on her bed. "It's not what you think. It's really not what you think."

"Try me."

"Dad, I can't talk to you when you're like this."

"Like what? I'm not like anything."

"You're all outraged parent right now. I can't tell you anything until you calm down."

"Don't tell me how to be. I'm the father. You're the daughter. Talk to me."

"Ash is a girl, and yeah, I go to school with her." Char paused a moment to let that sink in.

Her dad glared at her. "This is even worse than I thought."

"No, Dad, it isn't. You have nothing to worry about. It's over."

"Over? What's over? What was going on? Are you gay?"

"I, uh . . ." Char fell on her bed like she was about to pass out. It seemed so unfair that she had to have this talk when her heart had been crushed. "Yeah. I've known for a while. I didn't say anything. There was no point in saying anything until I met someone. I was going to introduce you to Ash. But now it's over before it even began."

"How can you know? You're so young."

"I just know, Dad. How did you know with Mom?

It's like that."

"But you're only seventeen."

She shrugged.

"What does Everett think of all of this? I always thought he was the one I had to worry about."

"No, you don't. He's a friend. And he, well, he doesn't know too much about this, actually. I mean he sort of knows, but he doesn't really."

"Who does?"

"No one. Just you."

"Good. Keep it that way."

"Dad!"

"Remember last year when you were going to quit school and go save the sea turtles? Or the year before that, when you were going to be an actor? Or even this whole YouTube thing you're doing now . . ."

"You know about YouTube?"

"I'm your dad. I know everything."

"What's your point? You think it's a phase?"

"Everything's a phase," he said simply. "Don't take that the wrong way. I don't mean to dismiss your passions. But it's true. It's all phases when you're growing up. And I'd hate to see you throw away your future because of a phase."

"Throw away my future? By being queer?"

"Don't put words in my mouth."

"But that's what you're saying, isn't it?"

"Char, calm down."

"Don't tell me to calm down," Char raged. "Don't tell me what to do. This is why I don't tell you stuff. You try to control me. But I'm not your little girl anymore."

"Don't I know it." He shook his head.

Char stalked out of the room. She went down to the kitchen and crammed some food into her mouth. And then she left. She got into her car and drove off. She didn't know where she was going. All she knew was that she couldn't be in her father's house right now.

Char was in a daze from lack of sleep. She stopped at the Krispy Kreme on Scott Road to get herself a coffee and a donut. By total reflex, she checked her phone and saw that Cinders was online. But that name had a different feel to it now. She closed her eyes and pictured Ash, the real Cinders. She felt how it had been to hold her and kiss her. It was so painful to think they were not going to talk anymore, to think that Char had lost her.

As she paid for her snack and coffee, she thought about sitting at a table. But she didn't really want to be in public. She looked awful. It was the first time since grade seven that she'd left the house with no makeup on. She was tempted to go to Shoppers and use all the samples to do her face when she caught glimpses of herself in the rear-view mirror. She had almost forgotten what she looked like without eyeliner. She hadn't worn makeup on the island. But there weren't mirrors all over there. And there weren't people around. This was different.

Char drove up Scott Road aimlessly. Maybe that was what Ash didn't like about her. Maybe Ash rejected her because she was too caught up in her own image. Ash didn't seem to care about style. She didn't have to. She didn't wear the latest fashion. She wore second-hand clothes and her jeans didn't fit very well. Her hair looked a bit like she'd cut it herself. Her glasses looked functional, not cool. But that was the charm. She looked like someone who didn't care about following fashion rules. And that's what made her stylish. That's what made her pretty. It was effortless. Ash didn't need to wear makeup because she had other stuff going on. When Char looked at her, she wanted to know what she was thinking, what she was going to say next. Char didn't look at her to judge her appearance. She wondered if Ash looked at Char — saw Char — the same way.

Up ahead, Char saw the recycling depot. She pulled into the parking lot. She just needed a place to stop and eat her donut. It was an apple fritter. Char hadn't had one in a while. She'd been watching her carb intake and trying not to eat gluten. Every extra bit of weight showed on video. One bite and Char didn't know why she bothered being strict with herself. She had forgotten the sweet rush of sugar and starch and fat. Life without donuts was not worth living. If Char couldn't have love, she could at least have fried dough.

19 Finding Cinders

AND THEN THE WEIRDEST THING HAPPENED. If Char was to tell it as a story later, she would say that magic was at work.

Ash emerged from the depot. She was wearing a scarf and her coat had the collar turned up against the wind and cold. Her hands were jammed in her pockets as she walked briskly across the parking lot. She looked like she had somewhere to go. Char watched Ash for a while. She felt stunned and unsure whether she should stop her or let her go. It felt wrong for Char to thrust herself on Ash. Ash had made it very clear that she wanted to be left alone. On the other hand, Char couldn't just do nothing. She didn't know what to do about how she felt so much for Ash. And now they both appeared at the same time in the same place. It was like fate.

Char started the car and drove after Ash, very slowly. She caught up to her and rolled down her window.

"Hey," Char called out into the cold.

Ash turned. "What are you doing here?"

"I hope I didn't scare you."

"You did a little. What are you doing here?" she repeated.

Char shrugged. "I don't know. Giving you a lift home?"

Ash stared at her.

Char tried to read the look on her face. It wasn't hate or disgust. But it wasn't pleasure either. Maybe disbelief? Char opened the passenger door. "Come on. Get in."

"I don't know."

"It's just a ride. No big deal. We don't even have to talk."

"Okay."

Once Ash was inside and buckled up, Char asked where to go. "Asking for directions isn't talking," she said.

Ash gave a little smile and told her the general area she was headed for.

"You were going to walk?" Char asked.

Ash nodded. "It's not that far. And it's easier on the way back because I'm not carrying a bunch of pop bottles with me."

"God. Not even the bus?"

Ash shrugged. "I'm saving for college. In case I don't get the scholarship."

"You'll get it, Ash."

"Don't be too sure about that. Competition is fierce."

"You've already got it. Your concept is genius."

"You're biased."

"So what if I am?" Char asked.

They both laughed. It was like the negative space between them had shrunk just a little.

"Char, I'm sorry for what I did last night," said Ash, looking down at her lap. "It was kind of messed up to lead you on like that and then run away."

"You did what you had to do. Do you feel different today?"

A sad expression settled on Ash's face again. "Nothing has changed. I can't see myself with you. I mean, you're practically high school royalty. I'm literally high school trash."

"I really wish you wouldn't talk like that," Char said. She gestured all over herself and made a small circle around her face. "This is so not royal."

"I think you look great without makeup. It's refreshing."

Char was surprised. "You think? I don't even feel like myself. It's so bizarre."

"You don't need it. I mean, there's nothing wrong with it if that's what you want to do. I'm just saying it's nice to see the real you. And in sweatpants even." Ash cracked a smile.

"Don't tell anyone you saw me in sweats," Char said, trying to sound menacing.

"Who would I tell?"

"I don't know. I'm being silly anyway. Sweats are comfy. I should really wear them more."

"Slippery slope," Ash teased.

Char laughed. "It would be a change from taking two hours to get ready every day."

"So maybe try it?"

"Yeah, maybe."

There was a silence. Char made herself wait it out. They were talking.

Finally, Ash asked, "How was the rest of your night after I left?"

"Honestly? The worst. But also kind of the best. I wrote a bunch of songs."

"Sad songs about what an awful person I am?"

"Yeah. Kinda." Char laughed.

"Can I hear one?"

"You really want to?"

"Of course. I didn't mean to be an awful person, just so you know."

"I know."

Char drove them back to Sunshine Hills. Instead of taking Ash home, she swung by her own house.

"Wait here," she said. She ran in, bolted upstairs, and grabbed her guitar. She was hoping she wouldn't run into her dad. Her good luck was still with her, and she didn't.

Char put her guitar in the back and got back in the driver's seat. "Where do you want to go? Can I take you to the beach?"

"Sure."

They drove in silence all the way to White Rock. Once they were at Centennial Beach, they parked and walked out in the rain. Char found a sheltered bench and gestured for Ash to sit down.

Char froze. Suddenly the whole idea seemed stupid. She could play her songs in front of a whole cafeteria full of students, even students who hated her.

That was fine. She could upload all kinds of stuff to YouTube and let the entire world watch her make a fool of herself. That was also fine. But to bare her soul in front of the girl who had already turned her down? That was too much.

"I can't do it," Char said.

"I'd like to hear it," Ash said softly. "For what it's worth."

"I'm nervous."

"It's okay," Ash said. She touched Char's leg. She ran her hand up and down Char's calf muscle. Suddenly, all the tension Char was feeling went away. Char took in a deep breath and she played. By the end of the song, they were both in tears.

"Will you play it again?" Ash asked. "And this time, will you let me record you?"

"Record me?" Char protested. "I don't know about that. Also, it's windy out here."

"In the car, then."

"Uh. Maybe."

They walked back in the rain. Char's hair flew all over the place in the wind. When they got in the car, it still smelled like apple fritter. Char looked at her phone. Her dad had tried calling her a bunch of times. She didn't know what to say to him, so she left it alone.

In the back seat, she played the song again for Ash. This time, she didn't cry.

20 Really Charming

ASH STOPPED RECORDING and looked back at Char from the front seat. "I'm sorry I freaked out last night."

"So you like me again?" Char asked. She set down her guitar and climbed into the driver's seat.

"Of course I like you. I never stopped liking you. I just thought you were too good for me."

"Why would you say something like that?" Char pulled Ash closer to her. Over the gearshift, they got really close, kissable close. Then Char whispered,

"You're everything I've ever dreamed of."

"Am I really?" Ash asked. "How come I don't believe you?"

"Because you're humble. Because you have no idea how amazing you are."

They kissed.

Ash pulled back. "Hey," she said. "Let's look at this."

She played the video recording.

Char felt a weird sort of shame. She wasn't at all camera ready. She hadn't spent hours on her hair and makeup like she did before shooting her YouTube stuff or for the showcase.

"I can't believe how pasty I look," she said.

"But listen to how you sound. Listen to your voice. It's the real deal."

"You really think so?"

"Char, you've got talent. I love this. And I shouldn't love it. It's about me being awful to you and walking out. I should completely hate it. But you make it sound so good."

Char knew it had to be a hard song for Ash to hear. But Char had poured all her raw feelings into it. Her suffering bled through every note. And her ragged look added to the effect. Looking rough might not be the worst thing in the world, Char thought.

"You should upload it," said Ash.

"I could, but . . ." Char felt a flush wash across her cheeks. She thought about the things people would say if they saw her looking like that. "I should redo it at home in a better outfit and better hair. Maybe put on some eyeliner."

Ash shook her head. "This is the real you. And it captures your sound beautifully."

"You don't think I look like a mess?"

"I love the way you look right now."

They kissed again. Char got caught up in being with Ash. She felt like Ash was able to show her who she was just by looking at her. Ash's gentle way of seeing the world gave Char courage. She had always felt judged by everyone at school and people she'd never even met before online. But now she found she didn't care in the least what other people thought. It was a brand-new feeling.

"You know what?" Char said. "I think I will post it."

Ash gave her a bright smile. It dazzled Char.

"What's that for?" Char asked.

"I'm proud of you," Ash said. "That's all."

As Char drove back to Sunshine Hills, they talked. They talked about school and all the things they wanted for after that.

Char wanted to talk to Ash about everything. She was intrigued by and attracted to Ash's mind and the way she thought. Char also felt really close to Ash emotionally. Ash was gentle, and that made her vulnerable in her own way. She was also strong and disciplined. But Char could tell that Ash was insecure deep down in ways that made Char want to protect her. Char drove along the highway and urged Ash to tell her more. More about her past. More about her thoughts on the future. Char hung on every word.

"I want to introduce you to some people," Char said as they got close to home.

When they pulled into the driveway of Char's house, her dad came out. Char knew he had been sitting by the window reading the paper, as he did every Saturday afternoon.

"Where have you been, Char?" he shouted. "I've been texting and calling. Don't you ever look at your phone? I thought you were glued to that thing."

"I was upset," Char said as she got out of the car. "I'm sorry."

Char was scared of what Ash would think of her dad. She saw him as if for the first time. He did not look friendly.

"Dad," Char said. "I want you to meet someone."

His face said it all. He did not want to meet anyone. But Char knew there was no point trying to deny anything anymore. She had to live her truth. Char felt a little sorry for him. Her dad woke up this morning with no idea about Char's queerness. Now, just hours after she came out, had to deal with her having an actual girlfriend. But didn't he himself always say that God acts quickly?

"Dad, this is Ash." Char gently tugged Ash forward. "She goes to my school."

"Oh, hello," he said. Then Char could see in his face that he realized where he knew the name from. He crossed his arms.

"She's coming in for a bit for tea," said Char.

"I think your mother is making dinner or something."

"Okay. Maybe Ash will stay for dinner."

Her dad said nothing. Ash turned to Char's dad and smiled.

"It's nice to meet you," she said.

"Mm-hmmm," he responded.

"Is that the new Apple Watch?" she asked.

Char's dad looked at his wrist. "It is."

Char said, "Ash invented an app. She's a genius at coding. She's got this idea for augmented reality on Google Glass. She'll probably get a scholarship for it."

Ash fiddled with a loose strand of her hair. "Char is being too kind. I don't think I'll get the scholarship."

"What's the idea?" Char's dad started leading them up the walk to the house.

Ash started talking. By the time they sat down to tea, Char tried to join in, but her dad was totally into talking with Ash.

21 *Fairy Tale*

CHAR KEPT CHECKING HER PHONE to see how many views her video had. Not a lot. She had received a lot of thumbs-up for the first hour. But now she was getting trolled.

Beneath her video, someone wrote "lesbo." It's not like Char had chosen her sexuality. She couldn't help but be who she was. And it was such a cheap shot it could have been done by only one moron: Mimi. It almost wasn't worth getting worked up about. *Who even uses that word anymore?* thought Char. Mimi had become so predictable that Char found it pathetic.

She remembered Ms. Merchant telling her how mean people try to hurt others to mask their own self-hate. She recalled how surprised she was when Ash had said that Mimi had her own problems. Char could see that Mimi would never have the kind of love that Char had found with Ash. So Char sat there staring at the word and tried her best to forgive Mimi.

But the slur bothered her. Hours passed and it was all she could think about. It was like Mimi had peed on her in public. It was like she wanted so badly to humiliate Char that she would stoop to anything. The dumbest thing about it was that it wasn't new. The song itself outed Char to the world. There was no need to comment on it, let alone write that word.

So Char did what she knew she could do.

Step 1: She called on the SendLove army. By the end of the day, the slur that had hurt her was drowned out by loving comments and cute emojis.

Step 2: When her alarm went off the next morning, Char already had her outfit picked out. She showered, shampooed, and conditioned. She put on her favourite lotion, the one that made her skin smell like pumpkin spice. As she piled on her jewellery, she thought about the chain-link armour warriors from long ago wore. She wasn't a fighter, but she wasn't going to let herself be vulnerable. Not today.

She styled her hair and applied perfect makeup. She drank the smoothie her mom had made for her. She drove to school and took a deep breath. From the driver's seat, she texted Ash a kissy face emoji with the words "see you soon." She struggled to squirm into her fitted leather jacket inside the Fiat and then lifted her bouncy dark waves of hair from inside the collar. She put on her sunglasses. She wouldn't need them inside. But they were lightly tinted and made her feel cool. She locked her car.

The heels of her boots made a click-clacking sound that she enjoyed on the walk up to the school. She burst through the front doors with bravado. Char would have liked it to be triumph, but the impression was just as important.

She breezed past the principal's office and the classrooms in the downstairs hallway. She headed straight for the cafeteria. As usual, Mimi and her friends were sitting at the table they had claimed as their own. They were drinking their morning coffees. When Mimi looked over, Char could feel her piercing stare.

Char had planned to ignore Mimi. But now she was there, she had a better idea.

Step 3: Char walked over to Mimi's table.

"Oh, hi," Mimi said. She was expert in that fake voice that made it sound like she was happy to be friends with Char. "How was your weekend?"

"Great, actually." Char's tone was cool.

"Oh yeah?"

"Yeah," said Char, loudly enough for the surrounding tables to hear her. "And for the record, it's not lesbo. It's lesbian."

Jaws dropped all around the table. Char turned on the ball of her right foot like she was a runway model.

She walked away like she was on a catwalk.

That was how it was done.

Char turned to see Ash working behind the cash register. Ash worked so hard that Char's heart filled with respect for her.

Ash saw Char looking at her and blushed. Char butted in line in front of a teacher without saying, "Excuse me," or asking permission. She put her hand out to Ash. Ash put her hand in Char's. Char brought the back of Ash's hand to her mouth and kissed it. The two girls smiled at each other while the teacher looked away.

Char didn't care who was made uncomfortable. She wasn't going to hide anything anymore. There was no reason to.

At lunch, Ash was working and Char didn't want to bother her. Char went to the cafeteria just to say hi. Then she and Everett sat together to eat lunch.

"I can't believe she's been right here all along and

you two never met," Everett said. "The whole story is just so unlikely."

"Yeah," Char agreed. "There's something magical about it. I can't explain it."

"You don't need to explain stuff like that."

"You're one deep dude, Ev," Char said, punching his arm.

He laughed. "Maybe pretty soon people will stop assuming you and I are a thing."

"God, I hope not!" said Char, pretending outrage. "I love having you as my beard."

"Yeah, well, it would be nice if I had a real girlfriend before graduation."

"Hanging out with a couple of lesbians isn't cool enough for you? Ev, you will look back on these as your glory days. If I were you, I wouldn't feel too sorry for myself."

He rolled his eyes at her. She laughed at him from behind a forkful of her salad.

Char left lunch early for music class. When she got there, there were no other students in the room.

Ms. Merchant had her feet up on her desk and was leaning back looking at her phone. When she saw Char, she smiled at her, but didn't take her feet down. *This is exactly why I like her so much*, thought Char.

"Oh, hey," Ms. Merchant said. "I'm exhausted. An old bandmate was doing a solo show last night. She asked me to join her on stage and we jammed. It was a lot of fun, but I drank too much." She paused. "I probably shouldn't have told a student that. Keep it to yourself, okay?"

"No problem," Char said to Ms. Merchant. "Guess what."

"Tell me."

"I wrote three songs this past weekend."

"Did you, now?"

"I did. And they were painful, like you said they would be."

"Real creation is never easy or glamorous, is it?"

Char shook her head. "And the thing is, I learned that I don't care about glamour. I don't care about looking good anymore. Or even about being popular or the number of views or thumbs-up or likes or retweets I get. None of that matters."

"I'm really glad to hear it, Char," Ms. Merchant said.

"Yeah. I was up almost all night, heartbroken and messed up. And in the middle of all that, these songs came. I don't want to sound flakey, but it was kind of spooky. It's like they wrote themselves."

"I totally get that," Ms. Merchant said, nodding. Then she looked sympathetic. "I'm sorry you're heartbroken."

"I'm not anymore."

Ms. Merchant chuckled. "That was fast. Must have been some really good songs."

"Just honest. And they got me the girl."

"I'm proud of you, Char."

"Thanks for teaching me to stick with it. Thanks for helping me to see what really matters."

"My pleasure."

Char laughed and was heading for her seat when Ms. Merchant said, "Hang on."

"What's up?" Char asked.

"You know I hang out at the Railway? They have this great women's indie music night, Chicks with Picks."

"Yeah?" Char had never been. She had walked by the place during daylight hours and tried to imagine what it looked like inside at night.

"The bartender who manages the place is a close friend. I showed her your showcase clip, just for fun. Because, well, I'm proud of you. You're my best student, you know."

"Really?" Char felt her cheeks get hot.

"Yeah, and she said she liked it. She wants to book you, if you're interested."

"Interested? I'd love to!"

"There's no money, or, well, close to no money. Just a part of what they collect at the door."

"Oh my God. A place with a cover charge? How cool."

"It's only five bucks. And I think it's pay-if-you-can."

"The money doesn't matter," said Char. "If I can play music for people, I'm totally in."

EPILOGUE

Happily

CHAR SAT AT THE KITCHEN TABLE. There were
recycled cardboard takeout boxes from Whole Foods
holding various kinds of food. For Char's family, it
was a typical Tuesday night spread. Everyone helped
themselves, digging into the organic salads, whole
grain pilafs, and noodle dishes.

"So, Mom, Dad. I have kind of a big ask," Char
said.

"What's up?" her mom asked.

"You guys were willing to pay my tuition if I got into UBC or Simon Fraser, right?"

"Did you get in?" her dad asked.

"Um, well, I did . . ."

"That's great!" they both said in unison.

"But . . ." She took a deep breath. "I don't want to go. I want to write songs and be an artist. I've been thinking about this. I need the world to be my classroom right now. I can't take any more school."

Clouds descended on the faces of both her parents. Her words were met with silence.

"You know I've been helping out as well as singing at the Railway," Char went on. "Ash and I have been talking about maybe renting a place together. So, well, I was sort of hoping I could use some of that tuition money for . . ."

"Bumming around?" her mom finished for her. "You want us to pay for you to live out some kind of hippie artist fantasy?"

"No," said Char. "I was just thinking a couple months' rent while we get set up."

Her dad looked down. He only said one word. "No."

"Char, do you really think we busted our hides all these years so that you could squander money on hanging out?" her mom asked. "Your dad and I work hard. Don't you get that?"

"I'd work hard too. At a job, not school. At learning how to budget and live on my own. At songwriting. At practising and getting better at my craft. Ms. Merchant thinks I have a real future."

"I don't care what some music teacher thinks," said her mom.

"Well, I don't want to go to UBC or Simon Fraser. I just don't. I'm doing this with or without you. I just thought you'd want the chance to support my choices."

"Education, Char," said her dad. "That's what we support."

"I don't want to do more school," Char said. "I want to do music."

"Music is a hobby," her dad countered.

"No," she said, surprised by the force of the word.

"Music is my life." She got up from the table, leaving most of her Kung Pao Chicken.

Char grabbed her keys from the fancy hook in the foyer and put on her sunglasses. She was already crying by the time she was out the door. Char drove straight to Ash's house and texted from the driveway. Ash came out right away and got in the Fiat.

Ash could see Char's tears behind the sunglasses. "What's wrong?"

"Everything. My parents are being jerks about next year. They want me to keep studying. And that's that."

"What did you tell them?"

"That I'm not. That we have plans. That I'm going to be a singer and a songwriter. That I'm going to make music, no matter what they think."

"Good for you." Ash looked confident.

Char wished she felt that way. "Yeah. But they have a point. How are we going to live?"

"Well, you're already making money bussing and cleaning at the Railway. That's on top of your share of the cover charge," said Ash. "And I'll have the scholarship. We'll make it work. I mean, it won't be deluxe or anything, but we can do it. My mom and I got by on a lot less than you'd think."

"I guess I could sell the Fiat. Mom and Dad gave it to me on my sixteenth, so it's mine." Char thought about it for a second. She wouldn't need the car if they didn't live in Delta. If they lived downtown or near Commercial or Hastings-Sunrise or somewhere like that, they could walk. "I wonder how much I could get for it."

Ash whipped out her phone to check. "About fifteen thousand. It would be more if it wasn't the colour of a pumpkin."

"Fifteen thousand is perfect."

"Are you sure?"

"About starting a life with you and pursuing a career in music? As sure as I've ever been about anything in my life."

"What if your parents totally freak out and disown you?"

"That'll never happen. They'll be mad for a while. But I'll win them over. I am Charming, after all."

Ash snorted when she laughed. "Yeah, you are."

"Can we do this, Ash?" Char asked, suddenly serious. "Your scholarship money would go much farther just for you. Do you really want my future dragging down yours?"

Ash's laugh had turned into a gentle smile. "I could be asking you the same thing, Char. You're doing the same work I was doing in the cafeteria. You're giving up your Fiat and your home. Will you give up online fame and being popular for hard work and little recognition? Will you give up your family, even for a while, for me?"

Char knew the answer before Ash had even finished. "Happily," said. And she sealed the word with a kiss.

Acknowledgements

To Kat Mototsune, editor extraordinaire, I am grateful for the many delightful and insightful conversations. Working with you is the best. To everyone else at Lorimer, thank you for all of the support with this project.

To Tony Correia, Andrea Warner, Billeh Nickerson, Jackie Wong, Cathleen With, Monica Meneghetti, Karen X Tulchinsky, Angela Short, and Shana Myara, you kept me going, and talked me through plot problems and life problems. There is no adequate thank you for your wisdom and support.

My besties from the olden days, Cecilia Leong and Elaine Yong, you kept me sane (relatively) in the midst of chaos. I'm grateful for my wonderful co-workers at Directions Youth Services Centre and the resilient youth who chat with me there; you provide endless inspiration every day.

To my mom, with her broken hip and speedy recovery, thank you for showing me mental strength and determination. To Maria Callahan, who put me in a cowboy hat and drove me across America, thank you for showing me what it means to have a musician's heart.